WINDY CLOVER

PARNASSUS' STORE

BLACK...

MEADOW

BIG WILLOW

FURRY CORNER INN

BLACKBERRY HOLLOW

BLACKBERRY HOLLOW

Written & Illustrated by Paul Peabody

Philomel Books · New York

With special appreciation to Pat Gauch,
whose editorial suggestions and encouragement made it all come together;
Kathleen O'Hagan for her sensitive work on the original manuscript;
Brother Andrew Colquhoun for his advice on Western Scots dialect;
and Paul who believed in it.

Published by Philomel Books, a division of The Putnam & Grosset Group,
200 Madison Avenue, New York, NY 10016. All rights reserved.
This book, or parts thereof, may not be reproduced in any form without permission
in writing from the publisher. Published simultaneously in Canada.
Book design by Patrick Collins. The text is set in Sabon.

Library of Congress Cataloging-in-Publication Data
Peabody, Paul. Blackberry Hollow / Paul Peabody p. cm.
Summary: All the animal inhabitants of Blackberry Hollow become involved
when Parnassus the bear, absentminded but amiable inventor, tries to get
Tom McPaddy the frog back to his home in Scotland.
[1. Bears—Fiction. 2. Inventors—Fiction. 3. Frogs—Fiction.
4. Animals—Fiction.] I. Title.
PZ7.P2998B1 1993 [Fic]—dc20 92–8968 CIP AC
ISBN 0-399-22500-5

1 3 5 7 9 10 8 6 4 2

First Impression

For Jo

Contents

Foreword

On a shelf of the Parnassus Jubb Country Store in Blackberry Hollow are several old-fashioned brown bottles. Each has a yellow label with these words printed on it:

> Directions for use—
>
> Pour into breezes
> Mix with meadows and blue sky
> Follow after

If you ask Parnassus, the burly bear storekeeper, what it means he'll tell you to take one of the bottles and see for yourself!

So all that is necessary is to find a meadow and some blue sky, take the top off the bottle and pour the contents into breezes just like the directions say. Then out come the prettiest gossamers, one after the other, filling the air with a silver flurry. They are the seeds of the thistle and milkweed that fly so easily from your fingertips, and zig-zag and tumble and glide at their leisure. It is very natural to follow after them, though should you have a great many busy, important things to do, and should you forget, there is always the yellow label to remind you. And who can tell where gossamers will lead you—to what hills and hollows, or what merriments and joys you will find.

Then, if ever you go back and tell Parnassus that now you understand the secret of his old-fashioned brown bottles, he will be very pleased. He will smile like the store-keeper who has given you the best of his wares.

BLACKBERRY
HOLLOW

I

Spring Things

It was morning in Blackberry Hollow. Early, early morning. A familiar whhhEEEZZee wound its way up from Cobble Creek. It was a wee sort of whhhEEEZZee—just what you might expect from a wee, bagpipe-puffing Scottish frog like Tom McPaddy.

But for Tom this was only a starter. He began shifting his pipes to a better position on his shoulder. Back and forth he moved on the stone where he squatted, whisking his scratchety kilt all about, getting into the spirit of it. He drew in an extra-long breath. One of his eyes squeezed shut. Then he puffed so hard the pipe in his mouth nearly popped right out! The next thing you knew there was a loud, steady, whining WHHHHHHHHHEEEEEEZZZZZZZEEEEE.

It wafted over the hollow to every nook and corner, and promptly reached Blackberry Knoll, a tiny hill in the open air that was the home of Jeremy Field Mouse, Esquire. Jeremy had dozed off just moments before under a sheath of bark and *had* been sleeping peace-

fully. The mouse tossed and turned as the long whining wheeze turned into a mourn-ful tune.

"Oh, not that again!" he squeaked in a peppery voice.

WHEEZEEEEEEE WHEEEZETY-WHEEEEEEEEEEZE WHEEEEEZE WHEEEEEEEEEEZE The frog piper was going all out now.

Jeremy sat up, pushing away the bark that covered him. He felt sulky and cross. He had always liked to sleep through the day and tend to business during the night, as is the custom with field mice. And he had always kept to that schedule until Tom McPaddy came to the hollow. Tom and that bagpipe.

"Every morning," moaned the mouse, "that boggy bellows wakes me up, just like an alarm clock I don't need!"

Then he began pulling off his cap—the cap he wore to muffle

the wheezes. But this day it wasn't doing much to muffle them at all. Of course, there was always his Turkish towel. Sometimes he tied the towel around his head and ears—on top of the cap—to keep the wheezes out. But, St. Oliver! Why go to all that fuss and bother now that he was so wide awake! Anyway, it probably wouldn't have helped—that dreadful sound was louder now than he ever remembered it. Tom's winter piping had been loud enough, but this early spring piping was the last straw!

"I might as well give up sleeping altogether!" Jeremy squeaked miserably, and he pulled on his cap some more. It fit tightly. Jeremy had to pull and pull. Out popped his ears. Then he gave an enormous yank. Off came the cap. And over he went, BUMP!

But what was this? It felt like something still on his head. Something rather like a pleasantly warm frying pan.

"Oh meeee!" he looked up with surprise and delight.

It was the sun! And, somehow, it felt different than it had the day before, or the day before that.

It felt good, very good. And when Jeremy looked down he could see the soft gold light sparkling in his whiskers.

"Just the right day to get out my fine spring coat," he murmured. "Splendid in fact!"

Now, Jeremy had a quantity of belongings, and he had a large leather valise to put them in. And since *stuffing* came very naturally to him, he had managed to stuff all his belongings into that valise. Sometimes he had to stamp up and down on it with his feet to fit everything in! Now, he seemed to remember his fine spring coat being somewhere near the bottom of the valise—so he began rummaging.

SWISH! flew a clothes brush! SWOOSH! flew a pocket purse! SWISH—SWOOSH—SWISH! flew this and that and everything!

"St. Oliver! Where is it?" Jeremy rubbed his eyes. It was the usual fuzziness, for Jeremy couldn't see at all well without his glasses—a fine pair of pince-nez. So he put them on and poked his head back into the valise. This time his paw went down immediately and he had his fine spring coat by the collar.

It was like meeting an old friend again! Jeremy had always liked its soft tan color, its large lapels, the two fine buttons just above the tails. He quickly slipped the coat right on over his pajama top.

"Mmmmmmm . . ."

It felt pleasantly cool and creakly. Jeremy smoothed down the front and brushed off the cuffs. There was that old light feeling about the shoulders, and a lovely airiness generally. He couldn't wait to wear it.

Jeremy hurriedly stuffed his pajamas and an assortment of other things back into his large leather valise. Then he put on his shirt, his vest, his black tie, his bowler hat, *and* his fine spring coat. And off he went in the direction of Blackberry Wood, twitching over pebbles and twithering under twigs.

WHEEEEEEEEEEE-
EEEZZZZZZZZZEEE-
EEEEEEE

Jeremy stopped short.
There it was *again!*

Paws fairly flew into ears.

WHEEEEEEEEZZZZZZZZZZZZZZZZZZEEEEEE-
EEEEEEEEEEEEEEEEEEEEEE

Oh, what a *nuisance!* For a while, in all his excitement over his spring coat, he had forgotten just *why* it was that he was awake at this odd hour in the first place. But now it was dismally clear. It was Tom and those dirgey pipes—Tom making Blackberry Hollow sound like that faroff boggy Scotland of his.

So off Jeremy scampered, paws in ears and in quite a state of agitation when, stepping into some rather tall grass, he accidentally tripped on a stone. BUMP over he went. And BUMP he landed on the ground.

"St. Oliver!"

He rubbed his nose and looked all about, squinting.

"Where are they?" he whispered helplessly.

He had lost his pince-nez!

Now, very close to the place where Jeremy was having these latest difficulties, there lived a modest and retiring gentleman, Mr. Kip the raccoon. His home was under a moss-covered rock in Thistledown Meadow, a place apart from the hollow's lanes and byways. Though it was secluded there, Tom's piping had awakened him, too. Being one who liked to be up early, however, Mr. Kip never minded the wheezes. On the contrary, they made his fur tingle. Today he had stopped to listen in the middle of breakfast as Tom played "McPaddy's Lament," one of the frog's more plaintive tunes. Plaintive, indeed!

It was still quite early, and Mr. Kip had his customary morning walk before him. He smiled at the prospect—such fine spring weather he had for it! Perfect, he thought, to try out his new entry journal with the leather binding and vellum pages that was to be his record of springtime in the hollow. But just as he started putting on his clothes, musing the while upon the merits of early rising, his fur suddenly stood straight out all over him, for he noticed a commotion by the Four Corners oak tree just a little ways away. Tucking in his shirt, pulling up on his knickers and down upon his vest, he went over to see.

In a moment he found Jeremy Field Mouse puttering frantically about on the ground, making a great fuss. Just as Mr. Kip arrived, down came the mouse's foot on something that went CRUNCH!

"OH! ST. OLIVER! ST. OLIVER! ST. OLIVER!" shrieked Jeremy, distressed almost out of his wits. "OHHHHHHHHHHHHHHHHHHHHHHHHHHHhhhh!"

The mouse stood there looking utterly wilted. He was quite sure he had stepped upon his only pair of pince-nez.

"Pardon me, Jeremy," inquired the raccoon, "but whatever is the matter?"

"Didn't you hear me *step* on them?" cried the mouse. "Didn't you hear me break them into a *million pieces?*"

"Break what?" asked Mr. Kip, bewildered.

"*Here.*" Jeremy pointed. "Under my foot." And then he put the sleeve of his fine spring coat over his eyes so he wouldn't have to face the awful truth.

Mr. Kip, not knowing at all what to expect, looked down to see. "You mean those *sticks?*" he asked.

The mouse made no reply.

"Well, it seems like a lot of bother over a few *sticks,*" the raccoon ventured.

"What—did you say?" came a muffled squeak from underneath the sleeve.

"Sticks, Jeremy."

Out popped Jeremy's face behind the coatsleeve, and a look of surprise and relief began to settle down to the very ends of his fine white whiskers.

"Then—it's—not—my—pince-nez?" he asked hesitantly, squinting at the ground.

"Oh, *that's* what all the trouble's about!" And without further ado, Mr. Kip applied himself to the search. It wasn't long at all before the raccoon caught sight of something glistening in the grass nearby.

"Just a minute," he said, picking the something up and fitting it carefully over Jeremy's nose.

"My pince-nez!" cried the greatly relieved mouse, "my very own pince-nez! Not broken after all! And now I can see again!"

Mr. Kip smiled.

"You certainly look in better spirits now, Jeremy," he said.

"Well, thanks to you, I suppose. Being able to see again does help," the mouse sighed.

Mr. Kip bent down once again to pick up Jeremy's hat.

"Here," he said. And he plumped it down on the mouse's head. "Now you ought to feel one hundred percent."

"That's very good of you, Kip," observed Jeremy, straightening his hat. Then he clasped his paws behind his back and pointed his nose up at the sky. "But I don't think a bagpipe wheezing at bedtime exactly makes for a hundred percent mouse." He frowned.

"What?" returned Mr. Kip. "What did you say?"

"Or a hopelessly stuffed valise," the mouse went on, his voice rising sharply, "or tripping over a stone, or losing my pince-nez! A hundred percent, indeed!"

As the two started to walk along together, Mr. Kip turned inquiringly to Jeremy.

"Have you noticed anything different about Tom's piping lately?" he asked.

"Humph! All that boggy bellowing!" Jeremy snapped back. "What do you mean, different? Why, my day is practically ruined because of it. I should be asleep now!"

"Yes, I quite understand," the raccoon sympathized, "but I mean something very—"

"LOUD!" Jeremy broke in desperately.

"Sad, *I* mean," Mr. Kip returned.

The mouse made no reply this time. Instead his gait became slow and grudging.

"None of the happy jigs he used to play, just those *awfully sad* airs," Mr. Kip added, not able to let the subject go.

Jeremy stopped walking altogether.

"Awfully *irritating* you mean!"

WHHHHHHHHHH-
HHRRRRRRRrrrrrrrr
WHHHHHHHHHHHHHH-
HHRRRRRRRRRrrrrrrrr

A new, unfamiliar sound broke the silence of the hollow. Mr. Kip and Jeremy looked at each other, twitching their ears.

WHHHHHHHHHHHHHH-
HHRRRRRRRRrrrrrrrrrrr
WHHHHHHHRRRRRRRRrrrrrrr

"What was that?" the raccoon spoke up first.

"A dilly of something, I'm sure." The mouse scowled. "This is a very noisy morning, I must say!"

Then came a smacking-the-water sound, and the whirring again.

"I think we ought to investigate," observed Mr. Kip, with growing interest.

"Yes, I suppose so," Jeremy replied, unconvinced.

"It is a perfect day to explore, Jeremy! A perfect day for anything," Mr. Kip said coaxingly.

Indeed, warm puffs of air caressed their faces, buds and new leaves whispered invitingly about their ears, and the green earth tempted their feet with its soft, cushiony carpet.

WHHHHHHHHHHHHHHHHHRRRRRRRRRRRRR-RRrrrrrrrrrrrrrrrrr

The sound seemed to be coming from Cobble Creek, at the bottom of the hill just beyond them; and Mr. Kip, with a long stride and no little curiosity, reached the crest of the hill first and peered down.

WHHHHHHHHHRRRRRRRRRRrrrrrrrrr

"Hurry, Jeremy, look!" he called back excitedly. "Do you see who it *is?*"

"First wheezes, then whrrrrrs, what next?" the mouse muttered peevishly. "Yes, I'm coming, I'm coming." And as he scampered along in his twitching, twithering fashion, he fussed with his pince-nez and fiddled with the lapels of his fine spring coat. Finally he arrived and looked over the bank in the direction Mr. Kip was pointing.

"Ohhhhhhhhhhhhhhhhhhhhhhhhhhh," Jeremy moaned, "not *this* on top of everything else!"

2

An Unusual Invention

On top of everything else, indeed! It was Parnassus, the hollow's burly bear storekeeper and inventor, down by the creek. Quite clearly he was *not* minding his store, and that usually meant one thing: he was off trying one of his newfangled contraptions. When he was out in this fashion, Parnassus had an assortment of store signs to let Blackberry Hollow folk know it, signs like: "Be back in ten minutes," "Gone for an hour," "Out for the morning," or even "Will return in several days." He was very absentminded, though, and often forgot to put the signs up. So if he was not at the store, you usually had to guess his whereabouts or when he would return.

Well, here he was now, obviously "out for the morning,"

with a fishing pole in his paws, and he was working it back and forth above the water with great furry earnestness, as if he might be on the verge of catching something. He was all expectancy. He beamed. Kindness sparkled in his eyes, and joviality crinkled in the corners of his smile. Whatever was he up to? If he *was* trying out one of those inventions of his, there was not a hint in his demeanor that the usual disasters might be looming, that things might go awry again. His assurance was complete.

WHHHHHHHHHHHHRR-
RRRRRRRRRRrrrrrr
WHHHHHHHHHHHRRRR-
RRrrrrrrrrrr went the reel.

Or was it a reel? It certainly didn't look like any reel Mr. Kip or Jeremy had ever seen before. It looked more like a can than anything else. And there was Parnassus turning a crank in the side of it, bringing in the line. To add to the mystery, a pail was hanging underneath the reel, or can, or whatever it was. So here was yet another container for something or other!

WHHHHHHHHHRRRRRRrrrrrrrrrrr   WHHHHHHHHHRRRRRRRrrrrrrrrr

Parnassus hummed merrily as he turned the crank and worked the fishing pole back and forth. And amidst all this exuberance, his tiny spectacles teetered, his wide suspenders stretched, and his white baker's apron flapped about him like a billowy sail on a very large mast.

"Good morning!" Mr. Kip called out to him.

"Frightful, you mean," complained Jeremy.

"Good *morning!*" the raccoon called, louder.

But Parnassus was oblivious to everything except his humming and his fishing.

"GOOD MORNING!" shouted the raccoon at the top of his voice. "PARNASSUS!"

The bear stopped what he was doing and looked up.

"Oh, hello, fellows, how are you?" he inquired pleasantly, his voice deep and rather husky.

Jeremy scowled.

"Fine day for fishing," Mr. Kip called down.

"Yes, yes indeed," the bear responded heartily. "Sweet potato's pulling well today."

"*What* did you say, Parnassus?" Mr. Kip scrambled down the bank as fast as he could.

The bear was now hard at work on the line. "It feels like a whopper," he announced cheerfully. "Apple's pulling well, too," he added.

"*What's* pulling, Parnassus?" asked Mr. Kip. He motioned to Jeremy, who was lagging behind doubtfully.

"Oh, apple," said Parnassus.

"And did you say sweet potato before?" asked Mr. Kip.

"Yes, sweet potato, yes—" The line went slack.

"Oh, oh," Parnassus sighed. "I think I lost him."

"Lost who?" asked Mr. Kip.

"Yes, who—apple or sweet potato?" scoffed the mouse.

But Parnassus was too busy reeling in to answer. It took the bear some time, for there was quite a length of line. He wound and he wound. Then all at once he gave a cautious yank, and the next moment he was dangling something large and round in the air.

It was nothing less than a pie!

As the pole bent round under the weight, Parnassus carefully maneuvered the pie so that it swayed back and forth inches from the noses of his friends.

"Are you getting whiffs of sweet potato?" he chuckled.

"Did you catch that in the *creek?*" gasped the raccoon, blinking.

"Don't be absurd, Kip." Jeremy poked him in the leg. He frowned at the pie through his pince-nez.

"No, pie's the bait," Parnassus explained. "I hook it on, and then I have to be very careful. It takes quite some skill to send a pie down the creek without getting it wet. Very similar to skipping stones on top of the water, I'd say. And if you skip the pie properly it lands upright—*and* floats thanks to my special floating pie plate. Then I just wait—"

"Wait!" Jeremy cried incredulously. "Wait for what?"

"Well," chortled the bear, "I can just imagine someone down there not expecting it—and then, all of a sudden, sweet potato! Apple! Blueberry! A tasty pie!" Parnassus paused to savor the idea. "Then, when I feel a tug on the line, I tug, too, but not too much. I'm glad when someone pulls the pie loose."

Mr. Kip and Jeremy looked at each other in astonishment.

Meanwhile, Parnassus removed the sweet potato pie from the line.

"Well, just suppose you were Bartholomew Beaver with his family of ten," the bear mused, "wouldn't you be happy to see a freshly baked pie come sailing along, all ready to eat?"

"But Parnassus," Jeremy quickly countered, "just suppose

Marcus Mudwig, that rogue of a turtle, came along and ate all your pies—and nobody else even got to have a bite!"

"Hmmmmmmmmmmmmmmmmm," murmured the bear thoughtfully, as if Jeremy had raised a very important point.

"But, Jeremy!" The bear suddenly perked up. "Just suppose it was Tom McPaddy somewhere by the creek, feeling sad and very chilly as he has been of late, and along came one of those pies right from the oven. Well, he could hop right on and get warm, and perhaps even go for a sail! That might be as pleasant a surprise as he's had since he came to the hollow so many months ago, don't you think?"

"Yes, maybe so." Mr. Kip nodded.

WHHHHHHHHHrrrrrrrrr Parnassus turned the crank of his reeling device, winding up some slack in the line.

"Say, that's a very unusual-looking reel you have there, Parnassus," observed Mr. Kip. "It *is* a reel, isn't it?"

"Oh yes indeed—and a flour sifter as well." The bear smiled proudly.

"A flour sifter!" exclaimed the raccoon.

"Yes," Parnassus went on. "It's a Flour-Sifting Fishing Reel—and, I might add, the first of its kind! When I wind the line in or let it out, I'm actually sifting quantities of flour in this reel-sifter can at the same time. As the flour sifts down, I collect it in this." Parnassus pointed to the pail attached directly underneath the reeling mechanism.

"So, while I'm engaged in pie-fishing," the bear announced majestically, "I'm also sifting flour for the next pie-baking session at the Parnassus Jubb Country Store! What do you think of that?"

Mr. Kip stared at the bear with fascinated delight. Jeremy, however, looked thoroughly skeptical.

"Now watch," the bear said. "Would you bring me one of those one-pound bags of unsifted flour, please, Mr. Kip?"

Parnassus motioned in the direction of a nearby tree where there was a quantity of small bags bearing the words FLOUR (unsifted), and a large bag bearing the words FLOUR (sifted). There were also a number of pies, a spare pole, and an extra Flour-Sifting Fishing Reel.

Mr. Kip went over and picked up a small bag of unsifted flour and carried it to Parnassus.

"Yes, that's fine," the bear said. Then he pawed the cover of the reel-sifter can and pulled it open. "Now, Mr. Kip, if you'll just empty the contents of your bag in here . . ."

Parnassus bent down, and the raccoon emptied the unsifted flour into it.

"While you're doing that I'll remove the pail from underneath the reel with the freshly sifted flour in it," Parnassus said; and he did so with a deft motion of his free paw.

"There now." The bear smiled. "And if you don't mind one more thing, Mr. Kip. Just take this pail and empty it into that large bag of sifted flour over there; then we'll be ready for some more flour-sifting-reeling."

"You don't say," scoffed the mouse.

Mr. Kip was back in a moment with the empty pail, and the two were now ready to observe the next step in the pie-fishing procedure.

"The line winds up inside the sifter," the bear continued, "and the flour makes the line very slick—very slippery—all the better for a good cast."

Eager to demonstrate the sifting mechanism, Parnassus started turning the crank.

WHHHHHHHHHHHHrrrrrrrrrrrrrr　　WHHHHHHH-HHHHHHHrrrrrrrrrrrr

Just then Mr. Kip and Jeremy became aware of something sprinkling all about them!

WHHHHHHHHHHHHRRRRRRRRRRRrrrrrrrrr went the reel, WHHHHHHHHHHrrrrrrrr

"What's happening!" cried the mouse. "Why, I'm turning white! Stop! Parnassus! STOP!"

"You forgot *this!*" Mr. Kip waved the empty pail about frantically, trying to get the bear's attention.

The two started vigorously pawing at their fur and clothes.

It was like a snow shower in winter, only it was a flour flurry in spring!

The bear suddenly looked down at his friends, then at the reel.

"Oh, I've done it again!" he said in consternation, shaking his head. Parnassus had indeed forgotten to attach the pail to catch the falling flour!

"I'm terribly absentminded about these things," the bear said penitently. "I'm awfully sorry." And he reached down with one of his paws and tried to help the two as best he could to dust away the flour.

"It's a blizzard!" the mouse complained dismally. "I'm all covered with it, and it *isn't coming off!*"

"You should see when it gets all over *me*," said the bear, trying to distract them and hoping for a smile. "Why, I look just like my polar cousins. . . ."

But neither Mr. Kip nor Jeremy seemed to notice what he said, so busy were they dusting themselves off.

"I guess I haven't had enough experience yet with pie-fishing and Flour-Sifting Fishing Reels," he tried again. "But I hope I'm improving—"

"Improving!" Jeremy suddenly exclaimed in disbelief. "Why, it's nothing but unmitigated bungling!"

Parnassus nodded regretfully. He laid his fishing pole on the ground and went over to the pies under the trees.

"It's time for the big cast of the day!" Parnassus announced triumphantly.

"Oh nooooooooooooooo," moaned the mouse, who was still in a dusting-off dither.

"How about this extra-large blackberry pie?" Parnassus pondered out loud.

"Blackberry has always been a particular favorite of *mine*," Mr. Kip piped up, still having dusting-off difficulties of his own.

"Blackberry it *is*, then!"

Parnassus picked up the extra-large pie, brought it over to his pole, and tied it to the line—but not too tightly—only enough to allow for casting and a bit of tugging, so that whoever found it could remove it easily. Then he picked up the pail Mr. Kip had emptied and attached it to the reel. This time there would be no flour spills.

"Yes," he said confidently, "everything is ready now. Say, you know, fellows, my first cast this morning went sailing to the musical accompaniment of Tom McPaddy's bagpipe."

Jeremy gritted his teeth.

Parnassus lifted the pole and its bait carefully over his shoulder. "And this cast," he added, "will go sailing to the musical accompaniment of songbirds. Do you hear them?"

Yes, the two nodded.

"Are you ready?" the bear called out.

Yes, they supposed they were.

"All right then. One, two, three . . ."

WHOOOOOOOOOSH WHEEEEEEEEEEEEEE went the oversized pie down the creek.

"Watch *out,* Parnassus!" Mr. Kip cried—for just at that moment the bear, in the midst of this particularly vigorous cast of such a large pie, stepped perilously close to the edge of the creek.

"WATCH OUT!" screamed Jeremy, but it was too late. The bear had lost his footing, and down he went.

SPLASH! And a magnificent one it was! Parnassus promptly disappeared into a great whirl of water.

As for Jeremy and Mr. Kip, they were altogether doused. And when the spray and splash had settled down to pools and puddles, there was Jeremy looking rather like a fire-cracker fizzling out.

"ST. OLIVER!" he sputtered.

Parnassus' soaked head appeared above the surface of the creek.

"Parnassus!" Mr. Kip shouted. "Quite a splash!"

"An unexpected pleasure!" the bear called back, paddling about excitedly.

"An unexpected disaster—*that's* what it is!" cried the mouse, shaking and wringing great quantities of water from his fine spring coat. "Look at this sticky mess. First flour! Now water! Do you see, Mr. Kip? It's *paste*. That's what it is, PASTE!"

Mr. Kip looked at himself with sticky-wet bewilderment.

Jeremy just glared.

"This has not been a good spring day at all! ST. OLI-VER!"

Then the mouse gave himself one last shake, stamped his foot on the ground, and scampered off in high dudgeon, the tails of his sticky-wet coat flapping limply behind him.

Meanwhile, Parnassus, still in the water, was enjoying himself immensely. Over and over he pushed his paw against the bottom of the creek, causing himself to rise and sink like a giant furry bob. He kicked water every which way. He turned over on his back and floated. Then he scooped up water with his paws and gave himself a shower.

"Well," he said exultantly, splashing all about with enormous furry enthusiasm. "I wonder why I don't do this more often!"

3
Major

The next morning Jeremy was up again far too early to suit him, and in his usual swivet. He had this, that, and everything to contend with, especially his bunched-up ball of a spring coat. He had bunched it up himself in a fit of enormous irritation on his way home from the pie-fishing calamities at Cobble Creek. Of course by now the flour and water had dried—hard—and the coat was a very stiff, crusty affair. Unwilling to part with it, however, he tucked it under his arm and went off twitching and twithering in his fashion through Alexander Possum's pasture, muttering an assortment of St. Olivers over the whole business. So preoccupied was Jeremy with all this that he neglected to look where he was going, and he almost stumbled over someone's hoof!

"Say, be careful, Jeremy," whinnied a rich, melodic voice. Startled, Jeremy squinted up through his pince-nez. "Oh, it's you, Major."

A big brown horse gazed down at the mouse. The horse had a white blaze on his forehead, and his ears poked proudly through the brim holes of a tall stovepipe hat. He seemed to be in constant motion, shaking his mane, whisking his tail about, hoofing the ground.

Jeremy promptly held up his coat.

"What have you there, Jeremy?" asked the horse, bending his head down to see.

"*This,*" the mouse announced grimly, "is my fine spring coat. Would you believe it?"

"My," whinnied the horse. "Whatever happened to it?"

"Pasted!" Jeremy snapped.

"*Pasted?*" the horse returned, confounded.

The mouse took one of the stiff cuffs in his paws and crunched it.

"With flour and water," Jeremy added testily. Then he set to work unbunching his stiff little bundle—or *trying* to, for it resisted with the stubbornness of a cabbage! As Jeremy pushed down on one of the tails, it promptly sprang back. And as he pulled on an arm, there was a cracking sound, as if it had sheared off at the shoulder.

"Say, would you like some help with that, Jeremy?" Major asked, extending a hoof.

"Oh, I'm afraid it's beyond help, Major," the mouse said gravely. He put his paws under the coat and lifted it up as if it were a piece of sturdy lumber.

"What do you reckon you're going to do with it?" Major asked.

"I haven't the faintest idea. I'm thinking right now of burying it."

The horse, quite perplexed by Jeremy's odd predicament, nevertheless wanted to be agreeable, and so he nodded his long neck up and down.

"Or maybe I should show it off—Jeremy Field Mouse, all dressed up in his *fine crumply mess* of a spring coat—letting everyone know just *how* things are going with him—" The mouse's voice rose thinly. He stopped and laughed a fretful little laugh.

"Wait. I have a better idea!" he said, staring wryly up at the horse. He scrooched the coat up into a ball again. Then he rolled it along the ground a few inches and kicked it. "How about a game of spring soccer, Major?!"

He then began kicking it in the most disgruntled way, every step in the manner of a tiny soccer player who has all the odds against him. And he went on kicking it over Possum's pasture until he was altogether out of sight.

Whatever Jeremy was feeling about pasted spring coats, it was still spring in all its budding glory, with mayapples like small green umbrellas carpeting the woodland floor. The beauty of the hollow was everywhere to behold, and Major thought of following after the mouse with a word or two about *that* side of the coin. And he might have done it, too, except that he had risen early this morning to go to Windy Clover Mountain, his favorite place to go, and he was keen on getting there. Windy Clover had the largest expanses, ideal for galloping, with steep slopes that his hooves could argue with. And from the trail he took to the top, almost every Blackberry Hollow landmark was visible: the Parnassus Jubb Country Store, its thatched roof a-twinkle with dew; Pebbles Lane, curling in and out of various knolls and crofts and ending, finally, at the Furry Corner Inn on the far side of the hollow; Slippery Dip Pond, by now quite melted and looking very blue; Cobble Creek, sparkling in the morning sun; Alexander Possum's apple orchard in blossom. And, above and beyond it all, mountain upon mountain, as far as the eye could see!

Sometimes, when the wind was right, Major could hear the wheezing lilt of Tom McPaddy's pipes, and he would stop whatever he was doing and try a sprightly clippety-clop in time to it. He had always hoped to find out about the Highland Fling from him sometime. He would have asked Tom about learning some Highland steps when he met him hopping up Windy Clover Mountain just the other day. But then he noticed Tom shivering. "Warmin' misself oop," the frog said in that froggy Scottish brogue of his. He had felt

more shivery than usual, he explained, and needed a "deal o' hoppin' " to get warmed. Hopping up Windy Clover—so far from Cobble Creek or Slippery Dip Pond—was a "deal o' hoppin' " to be sure!

But now Major had to get down to business. And business for him was a game he played with himself called "Chase the Hat." His strategy was to keep the hat on at certain times and let it blow off at others. That meant special commands for his ears: "Down ears," "Up ears." Ears bending down in brim holes helped anchor the hat on, but ears standing up straight meant that a strong breeze or a good gallop could send it sailing—and him after it. Major, however, was sadly out of practice. During the winter he hadn't commanded his ears to do much of anything except to rest and keep out of range of too much gossip.

So Major set about murmuring "Down ears," "Up ears," and was soon so deep in concentration, making sure his ears did what he told them, that he didn't notice at first what was happening on the trail below him.

For there, strolling along Windy Clover in a very jaunty manner, was Parnassus, looking quite grand. On his head was one of his recent inventions, his Daisy-Pot Topper. It was a felt hat with a daisy pot inside it. Whenever Parnassus tipped his hat to say good day, there was the daisy pot, with

the flowers just peeping out! And Parnassus was much grati-
fied to see the curious and delighted reactions of passersby
when they saw it.

Before he saw Major on the path above him, whom should
Parnassus meet coming along toward him, waddling in the
most careful and cautious manner, but Gwendolyn Goose.
She was carrying a large basket that was filled to the brim
with eggs. It looked quite heavy, and she was taking great
pains to make sure it didn't drop or spill.

Gwendolyn had on her spring poke bonnet and shawl. She
looked punctilious and proper.

Parnassus bowed to the goose
with fine old-fashioned
grace, tipping his Daisy-Pot
Topper and waiting eagerly
to see the expression on her
face when she saw what
he had in his hat.
"Good morning,
my dear," he
said gallantly.

But Gwendolyn didn't notice the daisies. And indeed, she seemed to be in a particularly pettish humor.

"*You*, Parnassus!" she scolded. "Where are my hot buns and crullers? Well, *what* have you got to say for yourself?"

"Hot buns and crullers?" Parnassus fidgeted.

"You know what I mean, Parnassus!" the goose hissed crossly. "You promised to have them for me to take to Arianna Magpie's this very morning. Don't tell me you've forgotten all about it? I just stopped by the Parnassus Jubb Country Store to see if they were ready, and not a soul was there—not a soul. And the door was wide open!"

"Oh my, you *did* say this morning, didn't you!" Parnassus replied with consternation. "Oh my, oh my." He shook his head sadly and pulled his spectacles nervously down to the end of his nose and then pushed them back again.

It was an awkward, embarrassing moment.

The goose stared hard at Parnassus. "Forgot all about them," she honked, "you absentminded silly."

Parnassus, utterly crestfallen, didn't know what to say or do. So he held on tightly to the Daisy-Pot Topper and then tipped it to the goose again.

Finally, still hissing, she caught sight of something. "Say, what have you got in there?" she asked in a more moderate tone. "Under *that*." She pointed with her free wing.

"You mean under my hat?" The bear brightened.

"Yes, under your *hat*."

Parnassus didn't say a word. He simply reached up with both paws, took the hat off his head very gently, turned it over, and held it out for the goose to see. And there were the white petals of the daisies, just peeping out. They blew back and forth in the morning breeze. There must have been all of five flowers there.

"Yes, this is my Daisy-Pot Topper, Gwendolyn," the bear announced proudly. He looked intently at her, hoping she would be pleased.

The goose, curious, poked her beak about, examining the whole contraption. "Well, I must say, I've never seen a daisy pot in a hat before!"

Her irritability was fast subsiding and she honked and hawed.

"But, Parnassus," she finally said with a smile, "it's really quite nice, you know."

Parnassus fairly beamed.

The bear, feeling a bit more secure now, and with his hat to hold on to, ventured boldly, "Gwendolyn, those eggs look heavy—can I carry them for you?" He put the topper back on his head.

"Parnassus." The goose cocked a skeptical eye at him. "Can I trust you not to drop them? Are you *sure* you can manage it?"

"I certainly can!" he announced valiantly.

The bear put out a large, helpful paw. He took the basket of eggs from Gwendolyn as carefully as he could.

"Now, my dear, lead the way," he said, pleased as Punch that he could assist.

Gwendolyn was quite pleased herself to be relieved of the heavy basket.

But just at that moment an especially brisk Windy Clover wind came along, picked up the Daisy-Pot Topper from the bear's head, and sent it spinning down the mountain!

"My hat!" Parnassus cried out. "Oh, there it *goes*—my Daisy-Pot Topper!"

"Watch out, you're shaking the eggs!" honked the goose very loudly. "I *knew* I shouldn't've—"

Parnassus watched his beloved invention rolling downhill rapidly farther and farther away from him until he could stand it no longer.

"COCOA AND GINGERBREAD BEARS!" he boomed, an exclamation he used during times of great stress. And he went bounding down the mountain as fast as his sturdy legs could carry him.

"MY EGGS!" honked the horrified Gwendolyn. "MY EGGS! Come back with my *eggs!* HELP! My *eggs!*"

Parnassus, in his sudden panic, had taken the basket of eggs right along with him down the mountain, and with

every one of his plummeting strides the eggs went bouncing about. Many of them broke in the basket, and others on Windy Clover Mountain, and a quantity all over the bear himself!

Now Major, hearing the commotion from the path on the mountain where he had been practicing his ear drills, galloped down at once. He moved double time when he saw Parnassus, for he was particularly fond of the bear. He always admired his boundless good intentions and rollicking attempts to carry them out.

"I'm coming, Parnassus!" he whinnied. "Don't worry— I'll get it for you! I like chasing hats!"

Parnassus came to a halt on a crook of the mountain. He waved gratefully to Major, who went by him so rapidly it looked like the horse was flying. But the bear shook his head sadly, for he could see his Daisy-Pot Topper still spinning farther and farther away. When he dared to look back in the direction of Gwendolyn, she was waving her wings about in frantic dismay. And when he looked down at himself he saw his newly patched pants dappled with egg white, egg yolk, and eggshell.

Galloping at full speed, Major kept a steady gaze on the hat—something he was used to when he chased his own stovepipe. But just as the horse thought he would catch up to it near the bottom of Windy Clover, it took a sudden turn into Alexander Possum's apple orchard, rolling on its brim into a maze of trees—every one of which looked like every other one. Somewhere among them Major lost sight of it.

"Oh, fudge and molasses!" Major muttered as he galloped along. "It's gone now!"

Stopping short and out of breath, he started wondering where he would look next when he saw, running toward him, Sally Ann Rabbit, Leo Fox, and Molly Barbara Mouse, animal children of the hollow.

"Hello!" the horse called out. "Hello!" The three were his favorite riders, and he shook a hoof to them in salutation. "Oh, say, did you happen to notice a hat anywhere around just now?"

The animal children, happy to see Major, stopped and looked at him. "Your stovepipe?" Molly Barbara pointed helpfully. "But you've got it on your head!"

Major smiled. "No, I don't mean this hat. I mean the one that belongs to Parnassus. It went sailing down Windy Clover a little while ago, and I just lost sight of it very near here in the orchard."

The apple trees were filled with the morning sun. Branches basked in it, their first blossoms giving promise of good things to come. And beneath, the quiet earth lay dappled in its winnowed light.

Major whisked his tail. "Listen, how would you like to get on my back and we'll go on a search together?"

A great deal of clapping followed that remark, for the animal children liked nothing better than a ride with Major.

"Hop on, then!" And the horse bent his legs so they could easily climb up.

There was much jostling, as usual—clamoring about whose turn it was to be up front, since everyone wanted to be, and Sally Ann Rabbit had scrambled there first. Then there was a merry jounce from Major that settled everyone and everything.

"Now, just a minute," the horse called up to them. "I'll give you a good ride, but don't forget to look for that hat!"

Yes, everyone agreed they would.

"All right, is everybody ready?"

Yes, everyone *was!*

So off they went with a bound, Major galloping fast for some excitement before the search began. But they had not gone more than a few dozen yards when the horse started slowing down and whinnying loudly, "Look out, look out!" In a moment Major had come to an abrupt halt.

Just ahead—right in his path—was Buckingham Badger, who was waving his arms all about in an effort to flag them down.

"Whooooaaaaaaaa, Majuuuuuhhhh, whoooaaaaaa," a deep voice drawled out.

Buckingham, a stout and stuffy fellow, was landlord of Blackberry Hollow's Furry Corner Inn. It was a place where only the furriest felt welcome. Buckingham Basel Bozworth Bunchcomb Badger (his full name) came from a long line of pompous badgers, and here he was, the very picture of pomposity, dressed in elegant spring clothes—green velvet coat, green suede boots, and walking stick—out for a stroll in the grand manner. Being the sort that liked to have the whole world under his paw, as the saying goes, he was feeling quite pleased with himself just then for having stopped the horse with such ease and dispatch. Indeed, he seemed to puff out with big badgerish importance.

"Majuuuuuuuuuuuuuuuuuuuuuuuhhhhhhhhhhhhhh!" Buckingham bellowed. "You're just the one I want to see!"

Smiles and excitement aboard Major quickly turned to frowns and silence.

"What is it, Buckingham?" the horse asked dubiously.

"Eh?" answered the badger, struggling to make out what he said. Being well on in years, Buckingham was hard of hearing and needed the aid of an ear trumpet. So he took one from his pocket and put it to use.

"What was that? Speak up!"

"I said what do you want?" the horse repeated louder.

"Jiggety-jog, jiggety-jog!" cried the animal children, eager for the ride to resume.

"Quiet up there! Quiet!" Buckingham waved his paw scoldingly at them. "Stop that racket!" He pulled the trumpet out of one ear—so he wouldn't have to hear them—and poked it into his other ear.

"Now, Majuuuuuuuhhhhhhhhhhh," the badger announced, "I'm in a ghastly predicament, simply *ghastly*."

The horse whisked his tail about impatiently.

"The annual spring gathering at Furry Corner Inn, Majuu-uuuhhhhhhh. Why, it's just three weeks from today. Been racking my brain how to deliver *so* many invitations to *so* many notables this year. Of course you know about our spring gathering. Such a gala! Such a smash! Such gabbing and gadding! Such swish! Such swash! Why, last year we had the renowned Barkis Beaver and Isabella Otter all the way from the next hollow. And so much to eat and drink it makes my fur tingle just to think about it. . . . But, I simply can't depend on Wellington Pony to deliver invitations anymore. He used to take them 'round. But I guess you know about old Wellington. . . ."

"No, I haven't seen Wellington lately," the horse answered.

"Of course you haven't, Majuuuuuuhhh—because he's not up and about as he used to be. Oh, he's a real lounger these days, I can tell you. He's at Furry Corner almost all the time now, either asleep in one of our comfortable chairs or just sitting around twiddling his hooves. But as for you, Majuuuuuuuh, you're an active fellow. How would *you* like to deliver those invitations for me? Well, what about it, what do you say?"

The horse said nothing.

"Come, come, Majuuuuuuuhhhh, enormously special occasion, the gathering, you know . . . and of course you're welcome to join us for some of it in return for the favor. How about it, eh? Anybody who *is* anybody will be there. General Jenkins Wolf, Sadduccees Muskrat, and all the rest. . . ."

The horse still said nothing.

"Well, think it over, Majuuuuuuuhhhhhh," Buckingham said, his head tilted proudly back. Then he noticed the animal children getting more and more restless.

"You up there." The badger suddenly pointed at them with his ear trumpet. And, in an attempt to distract them while Major pondered his answer, he called up, "What's my name?"

"Buckingham Badger!" they all cried together.

"No, I want the whole name!"

"Bucking . . . Hamhazel . . . Bozzing . . ." Sally Ann tried.

"Wrong!" interrupted Badger sternly. "Start over!"

"Buckinghazel Bozzingham . . ."

"Absolutely wrong!"

"I know! I know!" shouted Leo.

"What is it, then?"

"Buckingham Basel Bozzlebunch Badgercomb!"

"No! Absolutely NO!"

The badger's temper was beginning to sizzle, and he kept taking his ear trumpet out of one ear and putting it into the other.

"Buckingworth Backingham Bozzingbadger Bazelhazel!" piped up Molly Barbara, in another earnest attempt.

"No! No! NO! STOP!" shouted the badger at the top of his lungs. "This is an outrage!"

Then, very deliberately, he corrected them:

"Buckingham Basel Bozworth Bunchcomb Badger, if you please," he said haughtily. "And I await your decision, Majuuuuuuuuuuhhhhhhhhhhhh."

Then he dug his walking stick into the ground with remarkable pomposity and turned about. But just as he did so, Major caught the badger's coattail with his teeth, and Buckingham, who thought he was walking away, found he was walking nowhere, several feet in the air!

"Put me down!" he shrieked.

Whereupon the horse swung him 'round and dropped him

right down in the middle of everyone on his back. Leo Fox, Molly Barbara, and Sally Ann couldn't believe it! Buckingham Basel Bozworth Bunchcomb Badger, landlord of the Furry Corner Inn, right there in the midst of them!

"We're going for a ride, Buckingham!" cried the horse. "Why not come with us!"

And off they went at full gallop, first through a shadowy patch of Alexander Possum's apple orchard, and then out to the sunshine and up the mountain—up, it seemed, straight into the sky! And when they had reached the very top, back down they came, as fast as Major could go.

Well, no one has ever kept such a vigil at his post as Buckingham Badger did upon Major's back that morning!

For, not being used to anything at all like it, he continually called out warnings: "We're falling—steady now, steady!" "Heads down, feet up!" "Watch out, low branch!" "Help! Water there!" and the like.

Major, heading across one particularly impressive slope, whinnied the command "Up ears." (As the horse had been practicing ear commands for a generous part of the morning, he was now interested in trying it out in earnest, and this seemed like a golden opportunity!)

"Nonsense!" exclaimed the badger gentleman, not at all sure what Major meant, but, for Buckingham, a safe thing to say under any circumstances.

In an instant the horse's stovepipe whisked off his head and went sailing for a fare-thee-well.

"Catch it!" the animal children shouted gleefully.

"Catch *what?*" shouted the badger, while Major raced after the stovepipe, unsettling the entire company. Buckingham, reaching hastily for something to hold on to, grasped Sally Ann Rabbit's ears!

In almost no time the horse was neck and neck with his hat as it went toppling along the ground. He caught it deftly in his teeth and was about to let it go for another chase, but then quickly changed his mind. He swung his head around, passed the stovepipe to Sally Ann Rabbit, and started off at a very fast gallop across the hollow. In less time than you could say Uncle Thaddeus Jolly Jump, Major was at the front door of the Furry Corner Inn, all out of breath. He bent his legs to let anyone off who wanted to. Needless to say, Buckingham slid off promptly!

"There, and we thank you for your company," the horse said good-naturedly and quite out of breath.

The badger tried to collect himself. Having lost his walking stick, he swatted the air with his ear trumpet.

"A rowdy, Majuuuuuuh. That's what you are. A rambunctious rowdy! And I, for one, won't be needing your services."

Buckingham was extremely cross. He stood there looking

adamant and grim. Though, *really,* beneath a leaf and a petal caught upon his whiskers, there was the very slightest hint of a smile. And you might have guessed he hadn't minded the ride quite so much as he made out.

Then, back to Alexander Possum's apple orchard the horse and his little company went with a bound. The whole way Sally Ann Rabbit worked to pat Major's stovepipe back on his ears, though it wasn't easy, galloping along and jostling about as they were. But she knew the horse's commands, and she added a few of her own to help the hat-patting: "Up ears, Major!" and then "Down a little, ears," but "Oh, not that much, ears," "Oh, naughty ears!" "Now up again, ears," "Please be good, ears," and then it was "Down ears, Major!" Success at last! And when they finally arrived at the place they had met that day, the animal children slid off the horse's back—one, two, three—all protesting that the ride was over too soon. "Yes," Major nodded and smiled, but he told them he wanted to look some more for Parnassus' hat. He didn't want to give up, he said. He knew how important hats can be, and he hoped *they* would continue to look for it. Sally Ann Rabbit, Leo Fox, and Molly Barbara Mouse all agreed heartily that they would. Then Major tipped his stovepipe to his friends as they said goodbye to each other and went their separate ways.

Trotting over to the edge of the orchard and getting himself as close as he could to the spot where he thought the hat had disappeared, Major began his quest in earnest. He chose first a small gully, a likely place with rocks, moss, and furze that made captive nooks and crannies.

"It must be here somewhere." He stamped his hooves in determination. And he stamped again.

All of a sudden a flock of birds in the trees overhead, feeling the vibrations from his hooves even to the tips of the twigs, fluttered their wings. They chirped loudly, then rose and soared all at once. It was as if every bird in Blackberry Hollow was there swooping up and away. How high they flew and so quickly—too high for him to call out asking their pardon for having disturbed them. Higher and higher they went. Soon they seemed like one great plume the wind had caught and sent waving toward the clouds.

Major looked back down at his hooves that had shaken the earth. He scolded them with a whinny and told them to be more careful next time. Where he stood, a trickle of meltwater from Windy Clover Mountain had found its way, filling in ruts and hoofprints. He could see a reflection of sky in one small puddle, bright and blue.

If Major had not been scolding his hooves, he might never have found her—the small gray bird that had been left behind by the others. She was injured and lay on the earth just

beside him. All she seemed able to do was to lift herself a little with one wing pushing against the ground. The other wing appeared injured, perhaps in a fall. Major could see her heart beating hard against breastfeathers, which were soiled and matted.

He was careful with his hooves now as he moved them away from her, and then he whinnied softly down, "How can I help you?"

Fearful, she said nothing.

The horse decided to gather grass and hay and bring them near, making a kind of nest all around her. As he did so he noticed something singular and beautiful—her gray color was in reality a mixture. The white of the clouds was in her feathers, the blue of the sky, the brown of the earth.

And who can explain it, but while Major worked and kept watch over her, he caught sight of the very hat he had been looking for! It had lodged in a bush not more than ten feet away by an apple tree that was shining in the sun. The hat was badly frayed from the long, tumbling journey. And all that was left of the daisy pot the bear
had put inside was a bit
of crockery and a few
daisy petals.

But Parnassus will tell you of the day he opened the front door of his store when, to his great wonder, there on the threshold was the topper he thought had been altogether lost! Although the daisy pot was gone, in its place were wood violets, as lovely as any in the hollow, clear to the brim and spilling onto the ground. And trembling in their midst was the small gray bird.

4
Tom McPaddy's Tale

WHEEEEEEEEEZZZZEEEE WHEEEEEEEEEZZZEETTY WHEEEEEEEEEEEEZZZEEE WHEEEEEEEEEZZE Tom McPaddy was squatting on a rock at Slippery Dip Pond one late, golden afternoon piping a favorite of his, a tune he used to play in the bonny bogs of Scotland when the McToads, the McHoppitys, and the McPaddys assembled for a gathering of the clans. It was a tune that always brought back memories of fine times in the bogs—the music and dancing, the games, the comradeship. Indeed, a yearning had been stirring in him for some months now—a yearning to be with his wee Scottish friends, to go home again. Playing a tune like that only made the yearning all the keener. And now, while he squatted there piping and remembering and yearning, he felt a small shiver. The shiver increased. It increased so much that he let the pipes slip from his mouth and shoulders. There was silence. A long, sad silence. And then he shivered some more.

Suddenly, up in the air he went—red and black kilt billowing—down he came, and up he went again, hopping at a great rate. He went around Slippery Dip Pond once, and then

around it a second time, and he continued going around it—and in the strangest fashion. Sometimes he made little hopping circles, and then large hopping figure eights, and often as not, the most peculiar hopping zigzags.

For as long as he could remember, Tom McPaddy had been plagued by recurring chills. They were icy feelings that began in his feet and moved up until they reached his head and then came down with a terrible tingling. Tom hopped promptly—and whatever way he could think of—whenever he felt them coming on. Exercise usually helped to warm him; but what a nuisance, having to interrupt things and get on with this workout at a moment's notice!

The condition wasn't for lack of clothing, either. On the warmest days, Tom would wear his full Scottish attire: Tam, shirt, vest, jacket, wooly scarf, scratchety kilt, and knee socks—but the likelihood was that despite all these clothes he would still get the cold shivers. It was the cold damp bogs in his bones; that's the way the frog explained it. Lately, he'd been wondering if he hadn't become something of a cold damp bog himself, though he tried not to take that idea too seriously.

But here it was spring, and Tom—bundled right up to his puffling chin—was having the worst attack of chills he'd ever had in his life!

"Hello!" a voice called out. "Tom McPaddy!" It was Mr.

Kip, the raccoon, in the marshy vicinity. Mr. Kip had seen a flash of red and black kilt, and now the frog was out of sight. It had looked to the raccoon as though Tom must have hopped straight into the water. But that couldn't be—there wasn't a ripple-ring anywhere.

"Haaaavvveee aaa carrRRReee," croaked a burry, shivery voice.

Mr. Kip looked in every direction, but he still couldn't tell where the voice had come from. Slippery Dip Pond was at the far end of Thistledown Meadow, and a good croak like Tom's could go clear across it. He could be anywhere.

A flash of red and black again, and Tom was off hopping, this time right by Mr. Kip, who promptly went in pursuit.

All at once the frog stopped short. He squatted very still, his great marble-round eyes bulging. His mouth opened wider and wider. "Haaaaaavvveee aaa carrRRReeee foorr ooold Tooom McPaaaddy!" he wailed, and it was the shiveriest, burriest bit of froggy Scottish brogue you've ever heard.

Then off he went again, doing his best to hop away his chills. Mr. Kip followed right behind. This hopping-stopping business went on for several more minutes, until the frog hopped to a full final stop, turned around, and faced the raccoon squarely.

"Shivery, eh, Tom?" Mr. Kip ventured.

Tom McPaddy's eyes bulged more. "*Verrry* shivery," he

croaked. He reached into one of his knee socks and pulled out a smoking pipe. He tapped it on his shoe, then filled and lit it.

"Pipe's no much o' a warmer," he said, puffing in. A little red glow appeared in the bowl, and smoke started curling up. "But it'll do for a spell." The frog blinked.

"Well, I guess I knoo what ye're thinkin', Kip, aye, I knoo." Tom tightened the pipe in his fist as if to squeeze the very fire from it. "Ye've been wonderin' aboot this hoppin' o' mine today, haven't ye? Thinkin', it's Tom punct'al aboot his shivers; an' Tom punct'al aboot his warmin' up. Well, it's more than that."

The raccoon shook his head, puzzled.

"Somethin' much worse, Kip." The frog blew out a delicate wisp of smoke. "Noo, when ye're ten thousand miles from the bonny bogs an' ye're missin' every last parcel o' them, well, there's a homesick shivery feelin' ye get that's no like anythin' else."

"Oh, so homesick for Scotland are you, Tom?" Mr. Kip nodded sympathetically.

"Aye, an' it's *doublin'* my shivers, Kip. Rememberin' Kilklydoon—aye, home. I've had many a time thinkin' aboot it since I left, but it's gettin' the best o' me noo."

"What's it like there, Tom?" the raccoon asked. "You're the only one I know who has come from anywhere other than Blackberry Hollow."

"Ah!" Tom McPaddy smiled for the first time that afternoon. "Well, there's no' anither bog in a' bonny Scutland like Kilklydoon. Aye, an' such a puffin' band o' frog pipers there—well, ye scarce would believe it. Imagine if ye can, Kip, frog pipers as far as ye can see—a-coomin' along in their fine tartans, puffin' on their pipes with all their might 'n' main—it gives ye a wee bit o' the shivers whether ye're the shivery sort or not!"

Mr. Kip quite agreed with that! "Do you think you'll ever go back, Tom?" he asked.

"Aye, I'd give my *life* to go back, if there was a way—but never to go as I ha coom—'twas too much for me, that was!"

"How was that so?"
the raccoon asked.
"How *did* you come,
anyway?"

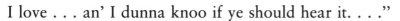

The frog shuddered. "Och!
'Tis a fearful fright o' a story,
aboot how I went off searchin'
for adventure an' left the land
I love . . . an' I dunna knoo if ye should hear it. . . ."

"I wish you'd tell it," Mr. Kip said eagerly. "I'd *like* to hear it—very much indeed."

"Well, let's do it soon, Kip, afore the shivers get the best o' me again."

The two found themselves a tree—one just right for sitting under and telling stories—and Tom leaned back, reminiscing.

"Well, Kip," the frog commenced, " 'twas like any ither mornin' in Kilklydoon, a wee bit chilly. I remember wakin' oop shiverin' as usual—thinkin' I'd had enough o' the cold damp bogs, an' that I should be oot tryin' my luck elsewhere— aye, seekin' adventure an' fortune. Often afore I'd considered it, but 'twas hard to make oop my mind, till that marn.

"I knoo of a ship, had been a dee or so moored at Wind- ledee Brae by the sea, an' I thought 'twas as good a chance as I'd iver have. . . .

"An' so, Kip, I went aboot packin' my pipes in a bag (an' a few ither belongins), took one last look aboot me, an' started off. It was a few miles to the harbor, an' all the way 'twas look here, look there at iverythin' for the last time.

"But there was nothin' like the sight I saw when I hopped o'er the crest o' the hill with the sea doon below. The sun was just risin' o'er the distant highlands an', Kip, the gold of it fell on the bonniest ship a frog ever hoped to see. Well, I'll tell ye, somethin' tingled right up from my toes to the tassle on my Tam.

" 'Aye, this is for me!' that's what I said to mysel' an' quick made it to the wharf—right in the middle o' swishin' ropes an' the heavy scuffin' o' sea-scarred boots. There I hopped aboot puffin' an' lookin' an' shiverin' an' likin' every minute of it.

"I' wasna long after, I heard a gritty voice tellin' us to be aboard the *Bonny Bannock*— an' we'd better be quick or be hanged! Well, Kip, I didna want to be hanged, so I dodged a couple o' boots an' tumbled into a skiff with some o' the crew.

I kept oota the way of them, hidden in the shadows under the bock seat—though I could well hear the talk o' the men. An' the more I heard, the less I liked; for they were a rough, grisly bunch. I didna relish the thought o' mixin' with the likes o' them.

"But I said to my-sel', 'Tom, ye have to take the briars with the bogs.'

" 'Twas no time our skiff was scrapin' the side o' the *Bannock,* an' I had to do some quick thinkin' how to climb the rope ladder no' seen by the ithers. But I didna have to think long for there was some riggin' goin' oop with one o' the sailors an' I went oop hidden in it. 'Twas lucky an' a good beginnin', I thought; an' I took one last look at Wind-ledee Brae, wavin' goodbye; aye, an' goodbye it *was!* When we reached the top I felt the boat swayin' under me; I heard the cries o' 'haul 'er oop' an' 'heave ho' an' the mighty squeakin' o' the tackle an' then I saw the white sails a-risin'.

"I knoo I couldna stay where I was, for sooner or later I would be seen. So I found my way to the hold—doon the ladder into the great dark. Wi' every step I could feel the chill o' that place go deeper in my bones; 'twas vast an' dingy an' damp. A shivery place as 'ere could be! Yet I knoo it was better there than gettin' in the hands o' that unsavory crew. An' 'twas doon there I stayed. . . ."

The frog stopped for a moment to light his pipe again.

"Och!" he continued, "besides the damp an' the dark, I had to put oop with a steady diet o' salt pork from the barrels, an' the everlastin' rollin' o' the ship. A few weeks o' that, an' I was gettin' weary o' it; I was itchin' for the sound o' the pipes. It had been a long time since I'd heard them. Yet I knoo if I played, the crew might hear them above, an' I'd be found oot; so I tried to content mysel' with joost thinkin' aboot the sound o' them.

"Well, Kip, have ye ever tried joost *thinkin'* aboot the pipes? It disna work! Soon I could restrain mysel' na longer. I started to play 'em soft, in a corner, where I thought naebody'd hear. I began 'Ere the Bonny Bogs Is Bloomin.' But I musta got carried away, for soon with its echoin' doon there in that great hold it began soundin' like the whole pipin' band o' Kilklydoon!

"I heard a great poundin' an' carryin' on at the hatch, an'

I could hear the raspin' voices o' the crew. 'Stowaway!' they cried. 'Stowaway aboard!' 'A stowaway piper!' Aye, and that stowaway piper was me, Kip! Och! Suddenly great hulks o' men started acoomin' through the hatch an' doon the ladder, first one, then t'ither! In the lantern light I saw their long eerie shadows, an' the face o' the one at the head—they called him Brass. He had a patch o'er one eye an' a wicked look in the ither. An' he says, 'Coom oot o' there, stowaway, who'er ye be, or we'll coom an' haul ye oot!' says he. I stayed quiet as ye can imagine. Well, my last hope, Kip, was that the pipin' music o' mine might hae soothed the savage beast in them (as the poet said), but, Kip, they were too rough an' grisly a bunch—only wantin' to get the stowaway, to catch 'im, to take 'im prisoner. Och, *me*, Kip, *me*. . . .

"I could feel the poundin' o' their feet on the boards like earthquakes as they coom closer. Then soodenly, my heart was like to jump into my gullet, for I 'eard one o' them say, 'O'er here, laddies!' An' pointin' to the place where I was!

"Doon came a boot, oop I went, doon came anither; then a shaft o' lantern light struck upon me! If one o' the men had looked doon at that moment, all would ha' been oop with yer old friend Tom McPaddy. But they didna.

"I joost drew in a mighty breath, as mighty a one as I could muster, an' with all my heart an' soul I began in again on 'Ere the Bonny Bogs Is Bloomin'!

"T'was the moment o' truth, Kip!

"'A BOGLE! A BOGLE!' one o' them shrieked. 'A BOGLE!' the ithers joined in. Well, they started runnin' an' jumpin' and jostlin' an' all the while shriekin' some more, 'A BOGLE! A BOGLE!' Aye, Kip, they thought I was a bogle hauntin' the ship 'cause they could hear pipes but couldna' see what was playin' them. T'was me, wee Tom, doon low. But och, doon low meant tryin' to dodge their flyin' boots to keep from bein' stepped on! T'was harrowin' that was, with

one close call after the ither. I tell ye, t'was like we'd struck a reef in the worst o' a Nor'easter! They were like a lotta big scared rats, goin' in every direction, some bumpin' into each ither an' into barrels an' trippin' o'er tackle; an' I kept right on playin' the pipes until every last one o' them was gone.

"But my trouble had joost begun.

"I could hear loud talk above, aboot how no one could see what it was playin' the pipes, an' how none o' them was puttin' oop with a bogle, and how there might be mutiny.

"I didna wish to be the cause o' mutiny, Kip! I stood there in that dark hold with some sharp wonderin' in me. I thought back on my peaceful bogs o' Kilklydoon, wishin' I was there. Then, with a leaden heart, I hopped across the boards o' the hold to the ladder to give mysel' oop—hopin' with all my soul they'd ha' mercy on me when I got oop there.

"I says to mysel', 'Tom, 'tis time. Ye moost walk oot bravely, wi' the pipes playin.'

"But I'd got oop aboot six steps when the ship jolted so hard I was knocked doon—doon an' doon until I hit the floor o' the hold. And it was a while afore I coom to, I dinna ken how long. When I woke I wondered what had happened to me. Perhaps 'twas a wave 'gainst the hull knocked me o'er; or we'd struck a reef; I didna knoo; an' still to this dee, I dinna knoo.

"Well, I couldna hear a whisper from above! 'Och, na it canna be!' I wailed. 'Twas mutiny, I thought, wi' none o' the crew left to tell aboot it!

"The hatch at the top o' the ladder was ajar, and I hopped back oop as best I could. Through the opening, I saw a ray o' the sun, Kip, after a' that time in the damp and dark, an' ye can imagine how I felt hoppin' oop to that hatch—aye, an' oot through it inta the bright oopen air, wi' the blue sky oop above an' the fair wind in my face! I heard the cryin' o' gulls, and it was a sweet, sweet sound, Kip. . . . *We'd come tae land!* I shall ne'er forget that moment, Kip—na, never.

"Many o' the crew had gone ashore, but the captain was walkin' along the deck, strokin' his beard. A coople o' sailors were talkin' o' tradin', an' I heard the captain shoutin', 'The spices . . . an' be quick aboot it!' They musta given oop the idee o' mutiny, I thought, 'cause o' the sightin' o' land.

"I was feelin' all the while how weary I was o' life at sea, an' how my bones ached for the feel o' firm ground.

"I hopped doon to the hold again, gathered my belongins, an' coom back joost as a great stout fellow went by draggin' a huge sack—movin' slowly, swishin' along. I said to mysel', *'If that's bound for land, then it's for me!'*

"So I hopped over to it an' grasped the bottom. Noo, Kip, I dinna know much aboot the ways o' travel, but I'll tell ye, there's one way ye dunna want ta go, and that's hangin' on to a sack o' pepper! For from oot that sack there was coomin' clouds an' clouds o' it, an' it set me a-sneezin' an' a-cryin' till I could hardly get a breath!

"Then that stout fellow picked us oop an' hauled us o'er his shoulder, cryin', 'Watch out below!' An' the sack an' me went o'er the railin'! I didna relish the thought o' landin' in the arms o' the sailors in the boat below, nor of the cloud o' pepper that would'ha coom oop in my face when we hit. So I jumped free o' the sack an' fell into the sea.

" 'Twas an icy cold shock, an' I had a shiverin' time tryin' to swim, but I had my pipes, an' joost the thought o' that kept me goin'. I made it to shore, Kip, an' it took me many a dee travelin', but that is how I coom to Blackberry Hollow, and I have been here ever since."

Mr. Kip drew in a long breath.

"But that isna the end, I fear," Tom McPaddy said slowly. "For 'twas joost a few weeks ago I was standin' on a rock at Cobble Creek, when in the water I saw—"

The frog stopped. His dark green color had gone quite pale.

"What is it, Tom?"

"It was mysel', reflectin' doon in the water," he said, shivering visibly, "but it was no' mysel' noo, but 'twas as I used to be back in the bonny bogs!

"I closed my eyes a coople o' times an' oopened them again. But always it was—he—*the ither Tom McPaddy!* An awful chill coom o'er me, Kip, for then there was a *voice,* like from far away, a voice like mine. . . ."

Tom, now shivering quite violently, rose from where he and Mr. Kip had been sitting.

"An' he said"—the frog paused, then went on—"an' he said, '*What are ye be doin' there, so far from your own Scutland, an' from the bonny bogs where ye love to be?*'

"And then it was as if a pebble dropped doon, makin'

ripples that started him highland dancin', roon' and roon' and roon' till I was dizzy with watchin'.

"Then he was gone altogither. I saw him nae more."

The raccoon sat silently, deep in thought.

Tom McPaddy slowly gathered his pipes and tucked them under his arm. He squared up his shoulders high and close to him; then he grasped tight to his scarf as if for ballast before a storm. All at once he seemed to swallow himself down with one last deep shivery croak:

"Soooo haaavvve aaa carrRRReee foooorrr ooold Too-ooom McPaaaady!"

Then off he went, hopping spiritlessly along Slippery Dip Pond until he was out of sight.

Time had passed quickly—more quickly than either of the two had realized. The pond was now glassy and still, and afternoon's gold had given way to the pearl and pewter of dusk. And as Mr. Kip watched his friend go, he wished he had done more than listen, that he could have helped in some way. Alas! Poor Tom. Poor shivery homesick Tom.

5

Parnassus and His Store

When problems pinched at the noses and tails of Blackberry Hollow folk, it was customary for them to pay a visit to the Parnassus Jubb Country Store. For in addition to the baked goods, pots, linens, quill pens, and other sundries always on sale, there resided the eager-to-please proprietor, Parnassus himself. The door was never locked, and even if Parnassus was out somewhere with one of his inventions, everyone knew they were welcome to enter and make themselves at home. If he *was* on hand and tending the store, he would always listen to anyone's needs, offer advice, or lend a helpful paw. Unless, of course, he happened to be pursuing one of his latest schemes. Then it was difficult to get a word in edge-wise.

The route to the store is an easy one: from Blackberry Woods you go north on Pebbles Lane, past Thistledown Meadow, over the stiles in Alexander Possum's pasture walls, until you reach the first fir tree. Make a right there and follow a gossamer all the way. It's not far, it never will be far. The store is tucked away at the very foot of Blackberry Hill—a lovely apparition of thatched roof upon white-washed stone. It was built years ago by Parnassus and his Grandpa Jubb, both devoted workers who were easily distracted by their own fanciful notions. Indeed, in spring they jumped into puddles, in autumn they juggled falling leaves, in summer they had honey holidays, in winter they took nap after nap. The job of building took them no little time. And being forgetful fellows as well, they admitted to having one day absentmindedly poured several dozen sacks of flower seeds and bulbs into the building plaster. And so, daisies, bluebells, primroses, tulips, and daffodils have been sprouting from the store's walls and ceilings ever since.

Over the entranceway of the store was a sign that read:

COCOA & Gingerbread Bears

CHURN HOME HOPPERS
SQUARE RIGGED ROCKING CHAIRS

Inquire Within

From the bottom of the sign hung the familiar Upside-Down Umbrella. One rainy day Parnassus had discovered that an ordinary umbrella, turned upside down, catches sparkling pools of fresh water. He considered the idea so monumental that he put one at the front of his store as a distinguishing mark.

"Yes!" the Blackberry Hollow folk complained, "right where you bump into it when you enter and leave—a terrible nuisance!"

Now, ambling up to the Parnassus Jubb Country Store this fine spring day was a preoccupied Mr. Kip. For Tom McPaddy had been on the raccoon's mind ever since he had heard his sad story. "It's Parnassus I must talk to," Mr. Kip was thinking to himself. "If anyone can help Tom, it's certainly our bear inventor."

The raccoon was just about to turn the handle of the store's front door when he stopped and twitched his ears. He heard music coming from inside. It sounded like a country dance, but it lasted only a moment, for it was quickly altogether swallowed up by an enormous BUUUZZ-ZZZZZZZZZZZZZZZZZZZZZZZZZZZZZZ!

It was hard to tell exactly what part of the store the buzzing sound was coming from, for it seemed to be moving about, and it became loud and soft by turns. Mr. Kip tried looking through the crisscross window of the bear's workshop to discover what it was. But he saw nothing. Then he went over and peeked in the bakery window. He couldn't believe his eyes! There was Parnassus, promenading back and forth in the midst of a great swarm of bees! At the same time he was, with the loveliest grace, playing away upon a violin. As he bowed the strings, bees buzzed this way and that all over him—from his paws to his ears, from his ears to his nose, from his nose to his cheeks and then all over his shirt and apron and then back for another buzzing round of it. A particularly buzzing bunch took a relish to the violin itself, while yet another buzzed heartily about the bow as it made its own buzzing sound over the strings.

"How extraordinary!" Mr. Kip exclaimed to himself, and,

"Oh, my!" He began tapping on the windowpane and waving in a warding-off-bees manner.

But the bear appeared to be so thoroughly captivated by the bee-buzzing and violin-playing that he didn't notice his friend at all.

Entering the store looked a bit chancy to Mr. Kip under the circumstances, but he *had* come to see Parnassus, and he *was* going to see him, bees or no bees. So he carefully made his way around the Upside-Down Umbrella, and through the front door, and then through the workshop all married about with carpenter's tools and curly shavings. With each step the buzzing sound grew louder, and Mr. Kip proceeded with extreme care as several bees buzzed by him.

Parnassus, now in the middle of the kitchen, was fiddling a lilting tune, bees following his every move with the greatest of bee-buzzing zeal.

Mr. Kip looked around for a safe place to stand. He saw the old black stove, hissing and bubbling, as mouth-watering whiffs of pumpkin, mincemeat, and chocolate filled the air. A pie cooled here, a pot rested there—pleasantly upside down. And there was that familiar sack from the pie-fishing, over in the corner—the one with the words FLOUR (sifted) printed on it. The raccoon moved gingerly into a corner by the stove.

Now, it was hard for Mr. Kip to believe that Parnassus

really wanted all those bees about him, especially during those times when he seemed more than comfortably swarmed upon.

"Parnassus!" the raccoon called, "aren't you *bothered?*"

Still just the bee-buzzing and the violin-playing.

Mr. Kip waited a few moments more and then shouted at the top of his lungs:

"PARNASSUS, AREN'T YOU BOTHERED?"

Enormous furriness thumped to a stop. Violin sawing unsawed. A large paw pushed spectacles up closer to wide, curious eyes. "Bothered, did someone say bothered?"

By this time the bear rather resembled a bush of bees.

"*I* said bothered," sighed the raccoon, stepping out of the corner and happy finally to have gotten the bear's attention.

"Bothered, Mr. Kip? On the contrary, I'm very happy to see you."

"No, I don't mean am *I* bothering you, I mean—"

"Why, Mr. Kip," Parnassus interrupted excitedly, "you're just in time to see a demonstration of my latest invention!" He held up the instrument in his hand.

"It's my Honeycomb Fiddle!" he announced grandly. "I had just run out of honey for baking, and that always means one thing—time for a tune! You see, there's a honeycomb inside—"

The bear pawed the belly of the instrument and out came a tiny swarm of bees from the sound holes.

"When I start playing," Parnassus explained, "it really starts things humming."

Mr. Kip nodded anxiously.

"Oh, I see you're concerned about all these bees," Parnassus said, gently shooing several dozen of them from the tip of his nose.

"Yes, aren't you bothered?" the raccoon wanted to know, relieved to finally make his point.

"Oh, bees are very friendly once you get to know them. They won't hurt you at all."

"Well, I'm glad of that," Mr. Kip said, a bit dubiously.

"Yes, and they usually make several pounds of honey an hour with some good fiddling." The bear smiled. "But let me show you!"

Parnassus turned the violin over, loosened a hook, and then lifted the back up on tiny hinges. Mr. Kip could see a honeycomb inside, and it was teeming with bees.

"There," said the bear. "Isn't that something!"

"Ye-es," the raccoon replied uneasily, "it certainly *is*."

Parnassus closed the instrument and set it down on the table. "I'm about to bake Miss Anne's cake," he said, "but the batter needs some more honey."

"Miss Anne?"

"Yes—the little white butterfly who lives down by the willow at Cobble Creek. It's her birthday this very day! And that reminds me, I'm going to need something else for that cake." The bear turned to his friend with a look of pleasant anticipation. "Mr. Kip, would you do something for me?"

"What is it, Parnassus?"

The bear led Mr. Kip into the pantry and to a small door. Over the door was a string of silver bells, and there was a cord attached to it, hanging down by the doorframe. Just over the bells was a sign that said:

BUTTER & CHEESE
(PLEASE RING)

"Would you mind ringing for me?"

"Ringing?" asked the raccoon.

"Yes. If you'd just pull that cord . . ."

Mr. Kip, although quite puzzled, agreed. He pulled dutifully on the cord, setting the bells to ringing.

Meanwhile Parnassus walked over to some shelves and began looking at the containers there, adjusting his spectacles all the while.

"That's right," he called back to the raccoon, "just keep ringing. We want to give them plenty of time."

"Give *who* plenty of time?" called Mr. Kip above the sound of the bells.

"Oh," said Parnassus, walking back over to the butter-and-cheese door, "the mice!"

"The *mice?*"

"You see," the bear explained, "they're probably having their midmorning snack in there right now. You can imagine how frightened they'd be if a big fellow like me came thumping in right at mealtime. Cheese is difficult enough to digest! Those bells give the mice notice that I'm coming. And it also gives them time to get a good supply of cheese before they scamper off. . . ."

The bear stopped talking and turned to Mr. Kip. "Thank you, and you can stop now. Quite enough ringing, I'm sure. I'll be right back!"

And then the bear opened the door and tiptoed into the butter-and-cheese room.

Soon Mr. Kip could hear the sound of something being poured and swished. That was followed by a creak and a clank and a hearty "There we are!" from the bear.

And in a few moments:

Clank, clink, clankety-clink

Clinkety-clank, clinkety-clank

It was getting louder and nearer.

Mr. Kip stood wide-eyed, waiting.

Clinkety-clankety-clinkety

Suddenly Parnassus burst from the butter-and-cheese room, clinkety-clanking up into the air, then clinkety-clanking down again. All about the kitchen he went, clinkety-clanking with great energy and purpose.

Mr. Kip saw that a barrel of sorts was tucked snugly between the bear's legs, with little platforms at either side for his feet, and a coiled spring attached to the bottom that kept clanking and springing Parnassus up into the air. The bear's paws held firmly to a pole that seemed to be going up and down through the center of the contraption. Mr. Kip thought that Parnassus looked like he was riding a merry-go-round horse that had somehow gotten free of the merry-go-round and was going grandly about under its own steam!

"What do you think of this buttermaker, Mr. Kip?" the bear bellowed as he sprang about the room.

"Is that what it is, a *buttermaker?*" exclaimed the raccoon.

"Well, it's really a churn," puffed Parnassus, "but I added a few things. You—probably (puff) noticed—the—large—spring (puff) attached—to—the—bottom (puff) (puff). Well, all this (puff) bounding about—helps to whip up a churnful (puff) good and fresh for Miss Anne's cake!"

Clinkety-clank, clinkety-clank

Parnassus brought the churn to a stop. "I call it a Churn Home-Hopper," he told the raccoon. "I thought of the idea last year while I was resting in my winter log. Now when some of the customers are wanting heavy cream for making

butter, I lend them the
churn for the trip home.
You can imagine what
a pleasure it is getting
over the countryside
in one of these. . . .
I guess you haven't
tried it yet, Mr. Kip!
By the time you're home,
you have enough butter for a week."

The bear bounced the Churn Home-Hopper up, down,
working the dasher vigorously. Suddenly he went springing
right over a chair, and then over a table, and then right
over Mr. Kip!

The raccoon clasped his paws protectively
over his head as he watched Parnassus
with a mixture of astonishment and
disbelief. The bear clanked
himself so high that
he could have
reached out his
paw and touch-
ed the store's
ceiling rafter with
no trouble at all.

Then all of a sudden the bear let out a most distressed sound of "Ohhhhhhhhhh" and "Ohhhhhhhhh my!" When he came back down, Mr. Kip noticed a look on his friend's face he had never seen before. It was one of deep sorrow and disappointment. Mr. Kip watched intently now as the bear went springing back up toward the ceiling again.

"Here on the rafter, Mr. Kip . . ." he puffed out of breath, calling sadly from on high.

Down he came with a clank.

Up he went springing.

"bird used to perch . . ." (puff, puff)

down

up

"her favorite place . . ." (puff)

down

up

"right by the rafter window . . ." (puff, puff)

down

up

"where she could see . . ." (puff, puff, puff)

down

up

"the sky . . ." (puff, puff)

Clinkety-clank, clink, clank . . .

Parnassus began slowing down. Clank, clink, clank.

And when the bear finally came to a stop, he had such a terribly sad expression on his face that Mr. Kip quickly came to him and said, "Parnassus, what is it, what's the matter?"

The bear slid off the Churn Home-Hopper and put his paws around it to steady it.

"Oh, oh, Mr. Kip, I'm just a silly fellow," he said, brushing at his eyes. "Don't pay any attention to me."

Mr. Kip looked at the bear with puzzled concern. "Tell me, Parnassus . . ."

The bear, holding steadfastly to the churn, asked Mr. Kip for a chair, which the raccoon brought directly.

"Thank you," he replied, "thank you very much." Then he sat down and leaned his chin on the top of the churn. A strange, faraway look was in his eyes.

"Yes, all right," he finally agreed. "Yes, I will tell you. It all began, I remember, on the day when Major came here with a surprise. He had found my Daisy-Pot Topper that I'd lost on Windy Clover. Kind Major.

I was so happy. But, do you know, he had brought something else besides. Nestled in the Topper was a new friend, a small gray bird.

She was badly off then and needed tending to. One of her wings appeared to be injured. Major had taken care of her for a few days but then brought her to the store so she could have warmth and refuge from the wind and rain. Well, I carefully took hold of the Topper's brim with both paws and brought the bird inside. I told her she was welcome here and that I would look after her until she was well again. I think she was pleased, though she didn't say so. She didn't say anything. She never chirped once. I suppose she was fearful of such a big furry stranger like me who thumped all about. But she must have known I meant well, because when I put her, topper and

all, in the warm corner by the stove, she looked content and went to sleep.

"A week passed. She lay there on her uninjured side and scarcely moved. It must have been terribly uncomfortable just staying in that same position all the time, and so I'd play my Honeycomb Fiddle for her, and Tom McPaddy would come by and do a Highland Fling for her. We must have been quite a sight—the two of us and all our antics. But they were attempts, Mr. Kip, to help her pass the long hours. I'm not sure she liked either the fiddle or the fling, but she seemed pleased with the attention. As yet she still hadn't spoken. Not until one morning when I thought I heard a chirp coming from the topper. I went over, and all at once she looked me straight in the eye and introduced herself! She said her name was Megan Gray. Those were her first words, Mr. Kip! I was overjoyed that at last she would speak to me, that she seemed no longer afraid. I told her what a fine name she had, that it suited her. I told her she was beautiful and would soon get well. And soon it was, she had shed some of her broken feathers and was sitting up almost straight!

"Then one day, thinking she might appreciate a change of scenery, I asked her if there might be some other part of the store she would like to rest in beside the corner by the stove. She said yes there was. And she asked to perch on the rafter, by the high window, where she would see the sky."

Parnassus stopped talking and pointed up to the ceiling.

"Right there, Mr. Kip, as I was trying to show you on the Churn Home-Hopper. Well, I said yes, she could perch there, on one condition. And that was that she come out to Thistledown Meadow with me and try out her wings first. Mr. Kip, she needed to gain more strength before perching on a high rafter! To this she agreed. And that was the beginning of our trips to the meadow together and sharing things out-of-doors. Always, we chose the prettiest patch of dandelions and clover as a starting place for our little exercise. I would put her on my shoulder, begin running a wee bit, and call out, 'Now, Megan Gray, now. . . .' And she would spread her wings (she could spread them quite well by then) and glide as far as she could. And I'd catch her. Though the flight was short and though it was only gliding—how we exclaimed over it every time she did it!

"But once, a few weeks ago, Mr. Kip, while we were sitting together in the grass out in Thistledown Meadow, something wonderful happened. She spread her wings and *flew*—from my shoulder up to my ear!

" 'Megan Gray!' I cried out. 'You *did* fly, didn't you!' And she sang back down to me, 'Yes, Parnassus, yes!'

"I must have clapped my paws together a hundred times!"

The bear, who had been holding the Churn Home-Hopper all this time, let it go to demonstrate the paw-clapping,

but seeing it start to fall, caught it just in the nick of time!

"That was the happiest day, Mr. Kip," the bear continued, "when she flew for the first time. And I was true to my word. She had proved herself and was stronger now. So I put her up on the rafter where she wanted to be. And there she spent—I don't know how much time—but it was many and many an hour just gazing at the sky. She longed to be flying, I know. Well, once while she was there by that high window, she did something quite daring. I was baking some of those pies for pie-fishing and was just putting one in the stove when I heard a loud chirp from the rafter. I looked up, and Megan was tilting forward as if she might fall. 'Back, Megan!' I shouted. 'Step back!' I quickly grasped both ends of my baker's apron and held it out like a net just in case. Well, *down* she came! But, Mr. Kip, she never landed in my apron at all! She spread her wings and flew! And, indeed, flew right back up to the rafter again with a beautiful grace! I congratulated her on her skill, but begged her not to frighten me like that again.

"Somehow, Mr. Kip, it never occurred to me that she

would ever fly away. But one day, when I looked, she was gone. She went somewhere into the sky she loved. Of course, I looked everywhere about the store, thinking she might be playing a game with me. But no. She wasn't anywhere. I suppose she's joined her flock by now. That's the way it should be, I know. But I've missed her—very much. Very much indeed."

Parnassus looked up wistfully at the rafter, but then gave himself a great shake. "I hope you'll forgive me for going on like this," he said, lifting his head and managing a smile. "And we must have a look in the Churn Home-Hopper, mustn't we?"

The bear pawed the cover. It came off easily. Then he and Mr. Kip peered inside. They could see the churn filled almost to the top with yellow, creamy butter!

"Some of this will be perfect for Miss Anne's cake," Parnassus said, and it was as if he had forgotten completely the sadness that had come over him just a moment before.

The bear walked over to his shelves and gazed thoughtfully at the containers there. He adjusted his spectacles and gazed some more.

"Now, this is peculiar," he mumbled to himself, "I can't even remember the right amount. . . ."

"The right amount . . ." Mr. Kip repeated after him, his voice trailing off strangely. For he was still thinking about the story Parnassus had just told him and of brave little Megan Gray.

The bear pointed to a shelf immediately above him. There sat two white porcelain jars with blue designs on them. One of them, the larger, had the letter *R* printed on it; and on the smaller one was printed the letter *F*. Both were labeled *baking powder*.

"I'm trying to decide," Parnassus said speculatively, "what size birthday cake to make for Miss Anne."

The bear stood still for a moment, pondering.

"You see," he told Mr. Kip, "this jar—the one marked with the *R*—holds baking powder that makes cakes *rise*. *This* jar"—and he pointed to the smaller one, marked with the letter *F*—"holds baking powder that makes cakes *fall*. Now, it's all right to use the rising kind for making *large* cakes—for someone, say, like myself—cakes that rise higher and higher till they're just the right size (and in my case, that means very big indeed!). . . .

"But I *couldn't* make a big cake for Miss Anne! Why, it would last a year or more, and get terribly stale! On the other hand, if I use the *falling* kind of baking powder, the cake might dwindle to the size of a crumb, and that wouldn't be much of a birthday cake at *all,* would it?"

Parnassus paused, and brightened.

"Of course, now if I were to use a little of the rising kind and a little of the falling kind, *together*—"

"But wouldn't that be like not using any baking powder at all?" asked Mr. Kip.

"Oh—I suppose you're right." Parnassus began to look puzzled again. *"Unless,"* he said, *"unless* there was just a little bit more of the falling kind than the rising kind . . . yes, of course!" And triumphantly he took down the two porcelain jars, put them on the table, and set to work.

"Now," he said, "we'll take a wee bit of Honeycomb-Fiddle honey, a little Churn Home-Hopper butter, some Flour-Sifting-Reel flour—and a very little of the rising baking powder—and a trifle more of the *falling* baking powder—yes, that should do just perfectly!"

Parnassus hummed as he stirred all these ingredients in a bowl not much larger than a thimble. Then he poured the batter into a thimble-sized cupcake pan and put it into the oven.

"You know, Mr. Kip." The bear turned to him. "I just realized I haven't asked you why you've come today."

But before there was any chance for the raccoon even to mention Tom McPaddy's name, Parnassus was walking ex-

citedly over to a string of cookies hanging up by the store's front window. The cookies had been freshly baked.

"Just like clothes drying on a clothesline." Parnassus smiled grandly. "Only they're cookies cooling on a cookie-line!"

Then, with a proud baker's twinkle in his eye, he bowed low and said:

"Would you care
for a gingerbread bear?"

Parnassus reached up and took one from the line and handed it to his friend. It looked ever so soft, sugary and inviting. Mr. Kip bit right in.

"That's just a taster," the bear announced with mounting enthusiasm, quite forgetting the question he had asked Mr. Kip just a moment before. "And now for the Parnassus Jubb Chocolate Jug! *That* would be just right for Cocoa and Gingerbread time. Let's see—now *where* did I put it?"

Parnassus walked over to a large closet with a sturdy oak door. When the bear opened the door, Mr. Kip knew immediately why it was made of such sturdy oak! For the closet was packed to the ceiling with pots and pans, all sizes and shapes—an incredible jumble.

"I just *might* have put it in here," Parnassus said, perplexed. "Sometimes I put the crockery in with the pots and pans. It's just possible . . . and oh, yes, here it is!" He reached toward the bottom of the pile.

"Under all that?" asked the raccoon with his mouth full, scanning the mountain of tinware. "Couldn't you use another jug?"

"Don't worry," the bear said confidently, "I'll have it out in no time." He took the jug by its handle and pulled as carefully as he could, but despite his pains the stack began to sway perilously.

"Parnassus," Mr. Kip warned, "it's pretty shaky. You might want to watch those pans on top."

"Don't worry, if they start tumbling I'll just close the d—"
CRASH, BANG, CRASH

Down came the pots and pans, one and all. And down went Parnassus with them, all in a great heap.

Soon the bottom of a shiny pot pushed up through the pile; then the shiny sides; and, poking out from underneath, a bespectacled nose. Mr. Kip thought the bear—with the pot on his head—looked for all the world like a furry, helmeted knight.

"Look," Parnassus said as victoriously as he could under

the circumstances. "Here, I have it!" And he brandished the Parnassus Jubb Chocolate Jug.

It was a lovely old bit of crockery, light blue-green in color, tall and slender, with pictures of gingerbread bears holding paws all around it. The word *COCOA* was printed on it, as well. And Mr. Kip noticed that in addition to the spout near the top of the jug there was *another* spout, near the jug's base.

A large kettle was whistling on the stove, and Parnassus brought it over to the table. He poured hot, steaming cocoa into the Chocolate Jug.

"Now, *that* is a *heavenly* smell," proclaimed Mr. Kip, inhaling deeply.

The two friends sat down at the table. They tied napkins around their necks, and looked with eager anticipation at the jug and at each other. Then Parnassus took a great quantity of gingerbread bears from a box and arranged them neatly on a plate.

"Have several," he urged Mr. Kip as he proceeded to draw thirty or forty of the gingerbread bears onto his own aproned lap.

The raccoon gratefully helped himself.

Suddenly Parnassus rose from the table. "It's spring," he cried, "and here I've forgotten the best part of all!" He hurried out the door, returning shortly with a pawful of spring flowers. Then he went right over to the Chocolate Jug and started poking the stems into the spout at the top.

"What are you doing, Parnassus?" inquired the curious Mr. Kip. "What about the cocoa?"

"Oh yes! The spout at the top is for flowers," the bear said, picking up the Chocolate Jug. "Now just hold your cup here by this one at the bottom," he told the bewildered raccoon.

Then he turned a little spigot and, sure enough, out came the cocoa, rich and chocolaty.

"Well, fancy *that!*" Mr. Kip held his cup with care.

"Yes, and what do you think of it, Mr. Kip?" Parnassus continued pouring.

"Why, it's—I don't know how you can . . . That's *enough!*" the raccoon suddenly exclaimed, for the cocoa was nearing the brim of his cup.

"Just think," the bear poured on dreamily, "if there wasn't a spout at the bottom, then we couldn't have spring flowers at the top—"

"Parnassus, it's spilling over the sides . . . Parnassus!!!"

"—and having cocoa and gingerbread bears wouldn't be *half* so merry!" Parnassus poured on in a reverie, oblivious to the rapidly forming puddle of cocoa that swept up three gingerbread bears, and floated them gracefully off the edge of the table.

Tinkle, tinkle, tinkle . . . the kitchen timer began to sound.

"Do you hear that? Miss Anne's cake must certainly be ready by now," Parnassus said, after the twelfth tinkle.

Mr. Kip was busily sopping up cocoa with his napkin.

Parnassus, so pleased with the prospect of the butterfly's cake being ready, scarcely seemed to notice the cocoa puddles about. He opened the oven door and peeked in.

"Aha, *just right.*" He beamed. He took a potholder in his paw and pulled out the tray. On it was the smallest cake you could possibly imagine!

The bear lifted the thimble-sized cupcake pan from the tray. He put a teacup upside down on the table, and onto it he gently coaxed the tiny cake from its pan. Then he took about an eighth-teaspoon of lemon icing and with painstaking care applied it to the top of the cake. One tiny, tiny candle fit nicely in the center; there wouldn't have been room for another one.

Parnassus put the cake on a shelf to cool. Then he turned to the raccoon and said, "Now, *what was it you came to see me about,* Mr. Kip? I hope you haven't forgotten, with all these interruptions."

"No-o," Mr. Kip said, and then he sighed. "Well, Parnassus, have you—ever felt—dissatisfied—with one of those winter logs of yours and gone looking for another, only to find that the one you had first wasn't so bad after all?"

The bear pulled his spectacles down on his nose. He listened intently as Mr. Kip told about Tom McPaddy, how very homesick the frog was, longing for Scotland and the bonny bogs, with no means in sight of returning there.

"And, Parnassus," the raccoon finished earnestly, "it seems he *should* go, but how? If there's a way, surely you're the one who can find it. Parnassus, what do you say? Do you think you could help?" His words had fairly tumbled out of him.

The bear appeared pensive. His ears twitched. He thumped the floor with one of his feet in a thinking manner. Then he walked over to the crisscross bakery window and looked out. His ears twitched again. He fumbled with his spectacles, then took them off entirely. But when he walked back to the raccoon, he had that special Parnassus twinkle in his eye.

"Mr. Kip!" He smiled hugely. "I think I have it. I know what we'll do!"

The raccoon breathed a sigh of great relief and satisfaction.

"Now, first Mr. Kip," the bear began, "I want you to take invitations to everyone in Blackberry Hollow. We're going to have an open house! And we must speak to Major about bringing some of the guests, especially Tom McPaddy, at just the right moment for a special surprise!"

Mr. Kip said he would do whatever he could to help, confident that a great plan was under way.

"Now, let me see," Parnassus pondered, clasping his paws behind him and pacing back and forth. "As for the invitations, they could say, 'Spring Open House at the Parnassus Jubb Country Store,' on such and such a date. 'Honored Guest: Tom McPaddy.' And, yes, I think I'll paste some of my colorful leaves on them to make them pretty, the ones from the cash register. . . ."

"Leaves?" Mr. Kip grew curious. "From the cash register?"

"Yes, dried leaves in the drawer compartments. I've saved so many of them. . . ." The bear looked all around him. "But I haven't seen the register lately . . . now, I wonder where I put it?"

"You've misplaced the cash register!"

The bear looked positively lyrical.

"Oh, Mr. Kip, you should see the maple and oak and hickory, all those colors together, and when I open the drawer they all come spilling out in the loveliest way."

"Out of the cash register? Don't you use that for pennies?"

"Pennies? Oh—I'm not sure, yes, I think there *are* a few, in one compartment. You know, I have favorite ones. . . ."

"Pennies?"

"No, leaves . . . the yellow ones—the ones that look just like golden stars. . . ."

6

A Mouse's Tribulations

Jeremy Field Mouse was on his way home through Alexander Possum's apple orchard one irritating afternoon when he spied Alexander Possum himself walking proudly along in his finest farmer clogs and overalls. Now Jeremy knew that Alexander saved those clothes for special occasions and never just went around in them, for clothing, his own and everyone else's, was always of great interest to Jeremy, and the mouse paid close attention to who was wearing what, and at what time.

A glimpse only minutes earlier of Buckingham Badger in his finest waistcoat and Sadducees Muskrat in high collar and cravat hadn't seemed particularly remarkable since they usually decked themselves out for everything in general, and it was hard to tell if it was for anything in particular. But when, somewhat farther on, Jeremy saw Gwendolyn Goose and Arianna Magpie both wearing their silkiest spring shawls and talking a mile a minute out in Thistledown Meadow, he became somewhat more curious.

And indeed, he wondered what the two were saying; but it was such a garble of honks and whistles that he didn't bother to listen.

The final straw was the appearance of Sarah Bunny Bristle, cleaning maid, and Sedgwick Fox, butler—both of Furry Corner Inn—who came strutting along in their Sunday best on this, a Saturday afternoon! Well, Jeremy realized that there was surely something going on in the hollow that he didn't know about!

"Excuse me," Jeremy began, approaching Sarah and Sedgwick with all the dignity he could muster.

"Who spoke?" asked Sarah, lifting her dress and petticoats to see where the voice was coming from. "Well, if it isn't Jeremy Field Mouse! Well, Jeremy, how do you do?"

"A MOUSE!" Sedgwick shuddered, for he was a skittish gentleman, and smaller creatures frightened him. "Get away! Shoo! Shoo!"

"My dear Sedgwick," said Sarah reprovingly, "but this is *Jeremy*—Jeremy of Blackberry Knoll."

"I just wanted to know what all the fuss is about today," Jeremy said, blushing, for the shooing had hurt his pride quite a bit, although he was intent on not letting that show. "Where is everyone going, all dressed up, you and everyone else I've seen?"

"Well, you don't look a bit ready yourself, Jeremy," remarked Sarah with matter-of-fact concern.

"Ready for *what?* That's what *I'd* like to know," the mouse asked with growing frustration.

"You mean you don't know?"

"Yes!" Jeremy stamped his foot.

"Yes you do or yes you don't?" Sarah queried.

"Yes, I don't!"

"Shoo! Shoo!" The squeamish Sedgwick was still trying to unmouse the premises.

"Stop that, Sedgwick," whispered Sarah sternly, for she knew how sensitive the mouse was and did not care to see his feelings hurt. "To answer your question," she said to Jeremy, "everyone is invited to an open house at Parnassus Jubb's."

"Everyone—Parnassus Jubb's? But—ST. OLIVER—why didn't anyone tell *me?*" The mouse gritted his teeth, fighting back tears, feeling thoroughly humiliated. "Why, that pie-fishing bungler, that—that paster of spring coats—" In his wounded rage, Jeremy stamped his foot on the ground again and scampered away—away from everyone—as fast as his legs would carry him.

It was some distance to his home on Blackberry Knoll, but at the rate the agitated Jeremy was going, he reached it in almost no time.

"An open house at Parnassus Jubb's, is it?" he was still grumbling miserably when he arrived home all out of breath. "And *me* not invited. I wonder *why*. I *thought* Parnassus *would* have—why—" And the mouse went on so, in low, worried, angry tones for several minutes.

Finally he took off his pince-nez and cleaned it with his handkerchief. He put it back on and glanced about him. He saw that something didn't look quite right about his over-stuffed valise, and his aggravation mounted.

Jeremy generally locked the valise when he left for the day. There were four locks: one at either end and two near the middle. Those at either end seemed now to be holding all right, but the two near the middle must have given way during the day—for a quantity of the bag's contents was spilling out there. Jeremy thought with dismay that his valise looked very much like a small volcano that had erupted.

"What a hopeless, bulging mess!" he groaned. He was quite hungry, but the thought of digging through the bursting valise for his supper pot was almost more than he could bear. He decided to postpone supper.

"I wonder what sort of an open house?" Jeremy muttered,

still thinking about Parnassus as he went over to his valise and picked a book off the top. It was called *True Stories of the Wee and Famous,* a favorite of his; and it did much to bring him comfort during trying times—so he always kept it handy.

"Ready for a little relaxation," he sighed to himself. "Yes, at last . . ."

He sat on the ground and leaned back, resting his head on a soft mound of earth.

Jeremy sighed again. He turned the pages of the book until he found his place. Then he began to read.

WHEEEEEEEEEEEEEZZZZZZZZZZZEEEEEEE

The mouse looked up very slowly.

WHEEEEEEEEEEEEEEZETY-WHEEEEEEEEZZZZE WHEEEEEEEEZZZZE

"It *can't* be! This is *too, too, too* much."

Of course, it was Tom McPaddy's bagpipes.

"That BOGGY BELLOWS!" Jeremy threw the book down, jumped to his feet, and rushed over to his straining valise.

"Where's my Turkish towel?" he cried out furiously. It was the towel he sometimes wound around his head to keep out the wheezes.

"Where is it?" he fumed, pulling out his bunched-up ball of a spring coat and sending it sailing.

"What's this?" He tugged, tearing a hole in the seat of his winter knickerbockers.

"That's not it!" Down came his fist on a hard pot. "OUCH! St. Oliver!!"

Jeremy picked up the whole valise and flung it down again. Out came everything that wasn't already out which, of course, included all sorts of items from the mouse's year-round wardrobe, and an assortment of cooking utensils, a gold pocket watch on a chain (this had belonged to Jeremy's grandfather) and an exquisite set of brushes with mother-of-pearl handles.

WHEEEEEEEEEEEEEEEZZZZZZZZEEEEE

In a final act of desperation Jeremy crawled into his emptied valise and turned it over on himself. And suddenly the mouse was aware of a remarkable thing: now he could scarcely hear the bagpipe wheezes!

He stood up and began to walk. The valise was heavy about his head and shoulders, making it hard to keep his balance. But such a thing could be tolerated, Jeremy thought, for peace and quiet.

"Say, what's going on here?" Jeremy heard a very faint, familiar voice from the other side of the valise. "Is that you, Jeremy?" It was Mr. Kip. "What on earth are you doing?"

"I'm under my valise," came a muffled squeak.

"Yes, well, so you are!"

Mr. Kip watched as Jeremy started walking, the valise swaying from side to side. Indeed, it looked to the raccoon as though at any moment the whole business was going to topple right over.

"May I ask *why* you are under there?" Mr. Kip had to yell right into the valise so that Jeremy could hear him.

"Must you?"

"Yes, I'd like to know!"

"Have you ever had your head in a valise, Mr. Kip?"

"No, I suppose not."

"Well, then, you've no idea
how things are in here."

"No, how are they?"

"Stuffy! That's how
they are!"

"Well, wouldn't you like
to come out?"

"No. This valise is the only thing that keeps the wheezes
out, and anything that does that is fine and dandy for me."

"Wheezes?"

"Yes, of that boggy, bellowing Scottish frog!"

"Oh, I see!" the raccoon exclaimed, finally understanding.
"Quite clever if it works. And rather quaint, I must say! But
Jeremy, this reminds me why I came here. There's going to
be an open house at Parnassus Jubb's store this afternoon,
and—"

"Yes, thank you, I've heard," the mouse interrupted cheerlessly. "Parnassus didn't invite me."

"But he *is* inviting you, Jeremy! You *are* invited. I'm the
one who's been going around inviting folk, and I came here

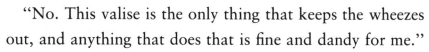

last because I was hoping you'd come
to the party with *me*. It's going to
be a very special affair, with
Tom McPaddy as the honored
guest," the raccoon finished.

There was a moment of silence.

"*What* did you say?"

"I said, it's going to be a very special affair, with Tom McPaddy as the honored guest!"

"That's just what I *thought* you said."

All of a sudden the valise plumped down on the ground. The mouse's legs and tail had disappeared altogether. But Mr. Kip could hear something—a rumpus going on inside.

"Are you all *right,* Jeremy?" He knocked on the valise and put his ear down close.

The rumpus stopped.

"Will you come with me?" He knocked again.

"Tom McPaddy, the honored guest, is it?" came the musty, muffled reply. "Yes, I'm coming, but *just like this!*"

7

A Bonny Farewell

Final preparations for the open house were going on in grand style at the Parnassus Jubb Country Store. Cocoa kettles whistled, newly baked gingerbread bears cooled, punch bowls glistened, blue-and-white checkered napkins cascaded, and stacks of shiny cups and saucers teetered. Parnassus was doing some last-minute decorating.

"Let me see." The bear glanced inquiringly all about him. "Now, where could I put a few more candles?"

Parnassus was most fond of candles, especially for festive occasions—and there were already very many of them, this late afternoon, on tables, windowsills, mantels, and whatever other tops of things the bear could find.

"Well, maybe that's enough," he said, seeing so many empty wooden candle boxes scattered about on the floor.

Parnassus found a broom and began to sweep the boxes into a big pile. Then his foot bumped into something. It was one of the boxes that obviously hadn't been emptied. Indeed, it had a very substantial feel to it—so substantial that Parnassus wished it had been the *broom* and not his foot that had bumped into it! He reached down and picked it up, immediately catching sight of two words lightly scrawled on the cover:

Umbrella Candles

"Umbrella candles," he mused. "Oh, yes of course! The very ones that belong at the front of my store!" Parnassus could scarcely contain his pleasure. Running to the door, he opened it, and ah!—there it was—his Upside-Down Umbrella hanging from the Cocoa and Gingerbread sign. A pool of fresh rainwater sparkled in it. Now it was going to be decorated for a special occasion!

Parnassus put the wooden box down on the threshold and looked inside it. Candles of every color greeted his eyes. Each of them had a hole in the bottom so they would fit securely over the ends of Upside-Down Umbrella spokes. The bear picked out a lavender candle first and fit it on a spoke. Then a yellow, a green, a blue, a pink. . . . When he had finished

putting on as many candles as there were spokes, he grasped the whole affair and started it twirling.

"Yes, my Umbrella Chandelier is going to look quite lovely all lit up at dusk," he said to himself, tilting his head first to one side and then to the other, "quite lovely indeed."

Then, just as Parnassus turned to go back into the store, he heard a crisp clippety-clop in the distance, coming closer. It was Major, bringing the first guests of the evening!

Oh, my! Parnassus looked down at himself, remembering that he was still wearing his apron, suspenders, and baggy pants. "And I was going to put on something special for the occasion," the bear sighed ruefully. He realized he had spent so much time decorating everything else that he'd forgotten himself! And by now Major had arrived with the first guests on his back, Grandmother Marjalene Woodchuck and her twelve grandchildren.

Parnassus sprang into action, offering his paw to help Grandmother Marjalene down, then reaching his arms wide to scoop down all twelve grandchildren at once! Major chuckled appreciatively at that gesture and was off with a bound into the hollow for more guests.

"Welcome, welcome everyone!" Parnassus exclaimed grandly and graciously. "Please come in. Come right this way."

Great excitement filled the air. An open house at the

Parnassus Jubb Country Store always meant something quite remarkable was about to happen. And judging by the way Parnassus was sparkling this evening, it was to be a most extraordinary something indeed!

The bear was standing in the doorway of his store, where he could easily direct his guests around the festive Upside-Down Umbrella Chandelier and into the room with the fireplace and the crisscross bakery window that looked out on Blackberry Hill.

"Be comfortable!" he coaxed them. "Have cocoa and gingerbread bears! Have punch and tea! Help yourselves!"

Guests were coming in numbers now, and the buzz of conversation was getting louder.

"My dear bear," a voice bellowed above the chatter, "and what sort of nonsense are we in for this evening?" It was, of course, pompous Buckingham. Parnassus smiled broadly and, without answering the badger's question, ushered him in with a flourish.

Gwendolyn Goose and Arianna Magpie came next, talking so much and so fast that they bumped right into Parnassus and lost a few feathers. Jennie Quill Porcupine, a bustling creature with a rather poking disposition, followed them (and very fortunately did *not* bump into Parnassus). Then came General Jenkins Wolf in tails, and his grand lady, Jessica Wolf, all frills and furbelows. Once again Parnassus looked down at his own suspenders and baggy pants, regretfully shaking his head.

Next, Alexander Possum came clumping in with his fine farmer clogs; then Wendell Weasel, a pointed-nosed fellow, who shook paws with Parnassus for a long time and wanted to know how long the open house was going to last, because he really couldn't stay later than six.

"That means you can stay until seven, cocoa-and-gingerbread time!" Parnassus replied heartily, showing Wendell in. Of course the delicious cocoa and gingerbread always enticed his guests into staying longer than they planned, to the bear's great satisfaction.

Next it was Sadducees Muskrat who arrived with a message from Wellington Pony that he wasn't getting around much these days and he hoped Parnassus would understand. (And Parnassus surely did.) Following him was a whole parcel of pompous ladies and fellows from the Furry Corner Inn. Although they preferred more sumptuous buffets and banquets than the bear offered, they always showed up for his cocoa and gingerbread—a treat, they insisted, that was never to be missed.

And following them came Mr. Kip in his best vest. He was steering a small leather valise that couldn't see where it was going—indeed that was twitching and twithering along quite erratically in front of him.

And finally came Major, this time bringing the honored guest, Tom McPaddy himself!

"Tom!" Parnassus hurried over to him.

The frog was holding on to Major's mane for all he was worth.

"We've been waiting for you, Tom!" The bear made a most gracious welcoming bow.

"And would somebody mind tellin' a poor confused frog what all the fuss is aboot?" asked Tom, all wide-eyed and windblown.

Parnassus assured him that this would be revealed very shortly.

Major bent down so the frog could dismount. "Haaaaaaaavvvvveeeeee aaaaaaaaaa caaaaaarrrrR-RRRReeeee." Tom shivered as he slid off the horse's back.

"Have a care, indeed!" returned the bear kindly. "Come in and warm yourself!"

Parnassus directed the frog through the front door, smiling his most benevolent smile, as pleased as he could be to have his honored guest at last.

"Thankee," the frog nodded, promptly hopping into a

cozy corner of the
sitting room—where,
judging by the sound,
everyone in Black-
berry Hollow was
chatting and sipping
and munching and
getting in the way
of one another's
bushy tails.

Gwendolyn Goose,
who had just sat down in
one of the Square-Rigged Rocking Chairs, was hissing and honking at a great rate (for there's no
knowing what will happen when you sit in
one of those! Indeed, it was used for Sunday
sailing trips high in the air!).

Parnassus, warmed to the heart by the
sight of it all, went about quietly lighting
the candles. And when he had lit the ones
in the sitting room, he went outside to light
the ones on the Upside-Down Umbrella.

"My Umbrella Chandelier." He smiled
and lit each candle with great pleasure.
Then he looked down in the pool of

rainwater collected there. Ah! Each candle's light was reflected in it. How lovely, he thought. Surely this was something everyone should see!

But now that everyone was here, it was time for festivities to begin. So he thumped his way merrily back into the store, calling for attention.

"My friends," he announced with great husky anticipation, "gather 'round!"

And he tapped a silver spoon upon his favorite Chocolate Jug.

Tap tap tap

"Say, pardon me," Alexander Possum interrupted, as he looked about for an empty chair. "Did anyone lose a valise? A very small one, on the floor here?" As the possum farmer reached down for it, he was met with vehement if muffled protests from within. It was hard to make out what the valise was saying, but it sounded rather like an assortment of St. Olivers!

"Well, fancy that," General Jenkins Wolf observed dryly. "A talking valise."

Tap, tap, tap. Parnassus spooned the Chocolate Jug again. Tap, tap, tap.

"Well, the special moment has arrived!" the bear said proudly. And he motioned with his paw for Penelope Bee, one of his Honeycomb Fiddle friends, to come over to him. Penelope, who had been quietly humming to herself on the punch table, started humming louder and quickly flew over to Parnassus' paw.

"Penelope has something to say," the bear remarked with a twinkle in his eye.

"Yes. Parnassus has asked me," she began delightedly, "to announce he will play a jig on his Honeycomb Fiddle as a prelude to the big surprise!"

"Play your *what?*" Buckingham Badger fumbled with his ear trumpet.

As Parnassus made his way through the company and out of the room, there was a great to-do, with everyone (except Mr. Kip) wondering what was to happen next.

In a moment Parnassus appeared at the door, his beloved Honeycomb Fiddle under his chin. "And a jig it is!" The bear came fiddling exuberantly into the room, while bees started swarming and buzzing excitedly all about him. Alas! The guests, fearful of the buzzing horde, scattered every which way. It looked very much as though there would be a jig generally and not from choice! Entreaties came from every quarter that the Honeycomb Fiddle be put aside in favor of some other kind of prelude.

Parnassus obligingly retraced his steps out of the room, fiddling all the way.

When he returned he was as unbuzzing and unbeed as they hoped he'd be. Except for Penelope, who was still on his paw. She immediately flew up to his ear and whispered to him in a very determined way. Parnassus nodded his head, obviously agreeing with her about something. Whereupon he picked up his Chocolate Jug and silver spoon and began tapping a musical tap, tap, tappety-tap, tap. Penelope, being a rhythmical bee, proceeded to do a jig herself for everyone to see. Tap, tap, tappety-tap. How she did go buzzing about

it! Tappety-tippity, tap, tap, tap. Well, everyone was delighted and said that a bee doing a Chocolate Jug jig could only happen at the Parnassus Jubb Country Store. As for Penelope, she told everyone that it was her tribute to Tom McPaddy and her own little prelude for the surprise to come.

Parnassus was now in the middle of the room, arms folded in front of him.

"Tom McPaddy!" he called out with great furry excitement. "Will you please come forward!"

"Tom McPaddy!" repeated Sarah Bunny Bristle. "Where are you?"

"And what may ye be wantin' with me?" Tom's voice brogued from under the punch table.

"You'll be seein' when ye come forward!" Parnassus brogued back eagerly.

"And will I be likin' it?" The frog poked his Tam-o'-Shantered head into view.

"I be thinkin' ye will." The bear gave him a big comforting smile.

"Well, here I am, then." Tom hopped out cautiously. His scratchety kilt whisked back and forth as he made his way over to Parnassus, his pipes rattling with every step, his eyes bulging with great froggy curiosity.

"We've heard," Parnassus began with real concern, "that

you've been missing home of late, and rather badly, too. Is that so, Tom?"

"Ye mean Scutland?" asked the frog, sorrow creeping into his voice. "Ayyyyeee, an' what aboot it?"

Parnassus unfolded his arms. His tiny spectacles glowed with the loveliest glints of candlelight.

"Will you please lend me your bagpipe, Tom?" he asked quietly.

"My pipe? An' what may ye be wantin' with it?"

There was a general stir among the company at *that* request, and much exchanging of glances.

Tom hesitated briefly, but then trustingly handed the bear his precious instrument.

"Now for the surprise!" exclaimed Parnassus.

But when the bear looked around at everyone sitting on the edge of their chairs, waiting eagerly to hear what he would say next, he thought he would create just a little more suspense. He would pretend to be his old forgetful self right at this most important moment.

"Surprise . . ." Parnassus fidgeted convincingly. "Hmmmm, *surprise* . . ."

"Parnassus, have you *forgotten* the surprise?" honked Gwendolyn Goose from the corner.

"Uh—let me see," Parnassus went on, raising his eyebrows and looking about blankly.

"Haaaaavvveee aaa carrrRRReee," came a shivery croak.

This was enough for Parnassus. "Oh, Tom," he said comfortingly, "of course I haven't forgotten. Follow me!"

The bear walked out the door, and the next moment everyone caught a glimpse of him through the crisscross window, heading rapidly in the direction of Blackberry Hill. The animals all hurried after him so as not to miss the surprise!

It was dusk. A wisp of moon hung brightly in the sky. The shadows were lengthening across Blackberry Hollow.

All eyes were on Parnassus as, halfway up the hill, he took some small corks from his pocket and poked them into the air holes of Tom McPaddy's bagpipe. Then he continued up the hill, and everyone followed close behind.

"Tom McPaddy," Parnassus called out on top of the hill. "Where are you?"

"Right at ye feet."

Parnassus looked down and smiled.

"Are you ready, then?" he asked. He put a tiny pipe up to his mouth, and for a moment it looked like the bear was going to regale the guests with a tune! Jeremy Field Mouse, looking out through a crack in his valise, cringed.

Parnassus began blowing. The bagpipe filled with air. But there weren't any wheezes this time, for the bear had stopped it up so no air could escape. The bagpipe expanded more and more, and Parnassus kept right on blowing.

"Parnassus!" cried Gwendolyn Goose. "What do you think you're *doing?*"

"Haaaaaaavvveee aaa carrRRReee," Tom McPaddy croaked.

The bagpipe was getting larger. And larger. And larger. Soon the bag was larger than the bear himself!

" 'Tis the end o' my fine pipe," brogued a small, shivery voice.

"No, Tom," Parnassus cried excitedly, " 'tis the first Scottish Pipe Flying Machine in history!"

"Flyin' machine?" The frog goggled at his almost unrecognizable instrument.

Parnassus kept on blowing. He blew until he could feel the balloon of a bagpipe tugging strongly at him.

"Yes, I think she'll take you all the way—to Scotland, Tom," the bear announced with great pride. As he looked up admiringly at the contraption, he thought this might be his most remarkable aerial invention, more remarkable even than the Square-Rigged Rocking Chair and the Baker's Apron Parachute.

"Now just one more puff!" The bear breathed in deeply.

And into the tiny bagpipe pipe he blew an enormous puff of air. But it was one puff too many. The tremendous pull of the Scottish Pipe Flying Machine picked up Parnassus himself and began carrying him aloft!

"COCOA AND GINGERBREAD BEARS!" he exclaimed in consternation, his eyes wide, at one hundred feet above the ground.

"Where do you think you're going, Parnassus?" honked Gwendolyn Goose.

"Haaaaavvvveeeee aaaaa caaaaarrrrRRRRReeeee . . ." wailed Tom McPaddy.

"*Do* something, someone!" squealed Sedgwick Fox.

And such a general confusion there was! Guests were screaming, scurrying, scolding, jumping, fainting.

But suddenly Mr. Kip pointed down toward the bottom of Blackberry Hill. "Look!" he cried with enormous relief. "It's Major!"

To be sure, it was the horse bringing Sally Ann Rabbit, Leo Fox, and Molly Barbara Mouse on his back. He was late bringing them, for they had been playing hide-and-seek in Alexander Possum's apple orchard and were difficult to find.

"Hurry, Major!" Mr. Kip called, running to meet him.

As soon as the horse saw Parnassus wafting helplessly, rising ever higher above Blackberry Hill, he quickly let down his cargo and galloped as fast as he could to the top of the hill.

Everyone stood waiting, wondering what the horse would do.

"Come *down*, Parnassus!" Gwendolyn Goose honked. "Right this minute!"

But the bear, desperately holding on to the tiny pipes of the bagpipe balloon, floated higher and higher.

"I can't come down." He hung cheerlessly. "I don't have my Baker's Apron Parachute. Goodbye, Gwendolyn. Goodbye, Major. Goodbye, Mr. Kip. Goodbye, Jeremy. Oh, Tom, I'm terribly sorry. . . . Goodbye, everyone."

All Parnassus could do was to dangle and kick his feet to no avail. Indeed, he looked like some bungling bear acrobat on a runaway blimp.

"Let the *air* out, Parnassus!" Major suddenly whinnied as loudly as he could.

Now, five hundred feet high, Parnassus rallied. "Did someone say let the *air* out?"

"Yes!" Major urged him on. "Let the air out, Parnassus, come down!"

The bear looked at the pipes. Yes, he supposed he *could* let the air out! So, while holding on to one of the pipes with one paw, he reached out with the other and tugged one of the corks. But out they all came! And the pressure of such a great quantity of air being released brought forth such a WHEEEEEEEEEZZZZZZZEEEEEEEEEZZEEEEEEEEZ-ZZZZEEEEEEEEZZZZEEEEEEEEEZZZZEEEEEZZZEEEE-EEEZZZZEEEEEZZZEEEEEEEZZZEEEEEZZZEEEEEZZZ that all the froggy pipers in all the bonny bogs tuning up together couldn't have compared to it!

As for Jeremy Field Mouse, he promptly St. Olivered himself and his valise all the way to the bottom of Blackberry Hill! Mr. Kip followed after as fast as he could, and when he finally caught up to him, Jeremy was just climbing out of the valise, dizzy and reeling.

"Are you all right, Jeremy?" the raccoon cried out.

"Not exactly!" Jeremy glowered, trying to get his balance. "Did you HEAR that??"

"Yes, of course, but don't you see, Jeremy, Parnassus was just trying—"

"STOP! Don't say *anything!*" Jeremy, trying to collect himself, looked quite frazzled. "My *valise*—I thought it kept out the wheezes, but it *doesn't*—"

The mouse picked the valise up and dangled it before Mr. Kip in inglorious defeat. "It *will,* however, carry *all* my belongings *away* from this *noisy, impossible* place! Mr. Kip, I am leaving, *henceforth* and *forthwith.* . . . I shall see you in a year, or perhaps in the next *century!*" Jeremy turned about in a huff and scurried away. He *did* leave the hollow in short order, just as he said he would. No doubt he did pack all his belongings into that bag. But Mr. Kip stoutly insists that he was gone no longer than a fortnight.

Meanwhile, Parnassus had begun drifting down in the direction of Thistledown Meadow. He was frighteningly high—higher than he had ever been on any of those Square-Rigged Rocking Chair outings of his. Luck was with him, however, for the contraption's escaping air passed through narrow pipe holes and so made his descent slow, if wheezing loud. Despite some bouncy air currents, he found the bagpipe balloon veering in the direction of the big willow tree in the meadow—the one with long, supplesoft branches that spilled over and down like some enormous haystack. "Ah!" the bear exclaimed to himself, "if only I can come down on that!" So while he held on to the tiny pipes as tightly as he could with his paws, he pumped his feet and swung them about strangely in an effort to jockey the contraption into position for a landing on that tree. Indeed, there was just enough light in the sky for many of the bear's awed guests to see him finally tumble into it and disappear amidst its myriad cushiony leaves.

Now Major, who had been galloping as fast as the wind to try and save his friend, saw where he fell and soon found him on the ground admidst a tangle of willow branches, shaking his head in great dismay, the limp and deflated Scottish Pipe Flying Machine at his side.

"Don't worry, Major," the bear mumbled, quite shaken.
"I'm fine, just a few bruises."

Then the two looked at
each other and said nothing.
Major was quite out of
breath, and the bear
appeared dazed.

"Are you *sure* you're fine?" the horse whinnied with great equine concern.

Parnassus didn't appear fine at all. In fact, he had the most disappointed expression on his face.

"Major, look!" The bear pointed to Tom's grounded bag-pipe. "Look! I've bungled everything!"

"No, you haven't," Major retorted firmly. "You've just demonstrated how well the invention *works*. What an excellent idea, Parnassus; I take off my hat to you." (With that, the horse doffed his stovepipe hat.) "If it worked for *you*, you *know* it will work for someone the size of Tom McPaddy! Here, get on my back."

So Parnassus picked up the pipe, climbed onto Major's

back, and off they galloped to the top of Blackberry Hill. Parnassus immediately dismounted and waved to all his friends—every one of whom breathed an immense sigh of relief to see him alive and apparently unhurt after his ordeal.

Of course, the guests became uneasy when Parnassus began poking corks into the pipes again and doing so with that same old inventor's glint in his eye. But this time, quite fortunately, he was careful not to blow too much, and he brought the balloon of a bagpipe to exactly the right size for Tom McPaddy. The bear asked Mr. Kip to bring him a basket and some pieces of twine from the store, which the raccoon promptly did; and then he tied several ends of the twine to the handles of the basket, and the other ends to the pipes. No sooner had he done that than Tom saw what a fine contraption it was—his own Scottish Pipe Flying Machine, indeed! So he lost no time in hopping aboard; and waving happily and gratefully to everyone. And then he caught sight of the raccoon.

"Thankee, Mr. Kip. I be thinkin' ye had somethin' to do with this, for 'twas to ye that I told my story, and to no one else."

Mr. Kip smiled and pointed to Parnassus who had just released Tom and the balloon into the air.

"Aye, kind bear," the frog brogued, "aye, ye ha made a wee frog's dream come true, an' I shall n'er forget it."

The contraption was rising slowly now, and Tom cast a glance over the company he was leaving.

"Oh, an' Major, thankee for that rousin' ride here this eve; 'twas a good deed ye ha doon."

Goodbyes, smiles, and cheers abounded.

"Tom!" Parnassus called up to him. "Can you still hear me?"

The contraption was quite high now.

"Aye," the frog called back down, "that I can!"

"I have it on good authority, Tom," the bear waved up, "good weather's ahead! Penelope Bee just told me. . . ."

"Aye, 'tis a fine spring eve to be sure." The frog waved back.

Parnassus was now waving with both paws—and waving for all he was worth.

"Oh, and Tom!" The bear's voice trailed off. "Tom, we'll miss you!"

But the Scottish Pipe Flying Machine was now out of earshot. Everyone watched as it floated still higher, becoming smaller and smaller until it was but a bonny wisp against the moon and the darkening sky. And as the guests began bidding each other farewell, no one noticed Parnassus, who was walking sadly down Blackberry Hill alone, for he never liked saying goodbye to anyone. A short while later, when he arrived at his store, the candlelight that greeted him was flickering and dim. Perhaps, he thought, it was his tears made it seem so.

But when he saw his Upside-Down Umbrella Chandelier, he opened his eyes very wide indeed, for there was a bird he knew fluttering its wings in the water collected there. And Parnassus saw it was the bird Major had found and whom he loved. And his heart skipped with gladness.

"Megan," he whispered. "Megan Gray . . ."

Parnassus picked her up on his paw and put her on his shoulder as he had done oftentimes before. Then he reached over and touched the Umbrella Chandelier, and the cord that held it to the sign fell free; and Parnassus took it and held it over his head, and the water from it came down in a great shower over the two of them and put the candles out.

"Such a silly umbrella." Parnassus smiled. "But it has brought us together again."

And so the bear and the bird went along with the Upside-Down Umbrella Chandelier, now right-side up, over their heads. Across the fields they went and into the deeps of the hollow, and up into the mountains and along the mountain paths, laughing and singing. And as they did so the sky seemed to glow more brightly.

"Look!" Parnassus said. "Do you see how the stars shine, how bright they are!"

And he gazed all about him in great wonder.

"Do you see, Megan Gray," he said happily, "the stars are lighting the umbrella candles for us!"

And in Blackberry Hollow, the animals still speak of that evening when Tom McPaddy waved a bonny farewell, and the stars were full of the strangest, loveliest of light.

Afterword

Mr. Kip did write his spring journal after all—so the Blackberry Hollow folk say. And he did use the leatherbound book with the vellum pages, though it seemed he would never get to it, so busy was he in the affairs of his friends. But when spring ended and summer came, they say he went off on his own, sat down under the big willow tree in Thistledown Meadow, and wrote this entire love story in it—else we wouldn't have known it ever happened.